HE MUST GET AWAY. THEY HAD TRIED TO KILL HIM ONCE, AND WOULD TRY AGAIN.

He felt as a hunted animal must feel, frantically fleeing, aimless in direction, but running as long as he could move.

He saw the broken rocks ahead, and turned toward that area. There he might find a hiding place, concealment in which to rest a little while. He scrambled into a crevice and rolled beneath an overhanging slab of stone.

His ears were filled with a roaring sound and his vision was blurred and indistinct. He closed his eyes. Was this how it felt to die? It took a few moments to realize that part of the sound was not inside his head, but in the crevice with him. The buzzing sound was familiar, somehow. He had heard it before. It was like the rustle of dry leaves, like . . . he opened his eyes, startled. Like the buzzing rattle of a real-snake.

# The Flower in the Mountains

>>>>>>>>>>>>>>>>>>>>>>>

DON COLDSMITH

BANTAM BOOKS
NEW YORK · TORONTO · LONDON · SYDNEY · AUCKLAND

This edition contains the complete text
of the original hardcover edition.
NOT ONE WORD HAS BEEN OMITTED.

THE FLOWER IN THE MOUNTAINS
A Bantam Book / published by arrangement with
Doubleday

PRINTING HISTORY
Doubleday edition published September 1988
Bantam edition / July 1990

ISBN 0-553-28538-6

Published simultaneously in the United States and Canada

Bantam Books are published by Bantam Books, a division of
Bantam Doubleday Dell Publishing Group, Inc. Its trademark,
consisting of the words "Bantam Books" and the portrayal of a
rooster, is Registered in U.S. Patent and Trademark Office and in
other countries. Marca Registrada. Bantam Books, 666 Fifth
Avenue, New York, New York 10103.

PRINTED IN THE UNITED STATES OF AMERICA

RAD      0 9 8 7 6 5 4 3 2 1

Time period: Early 1660s,
shortly after *The Medicine Knife*.
Number 13 of the Spanish Bit Saga

# The
# Flower
# in the
# Mountains
»»»»»»»»»»»

# 1

\>\> \>\> \>\>

**H**e looked down, confusedly wondering where he was, as a person does when he awakens in a strange place. In the dim light, he attempted to remember his surroundings. The effort was unsuccessful. He had no memory of any of the persons and things that met his gaze.

He was looking down into a circular enclosure, a lodge of some sort. Not a lodge of skins, but a round hole or pit, dug into the ground. Several people were there, grouped around a prostrate figure on a robe or mat. There appeared to be a ceremony in progress. One man, apparently a medicine man, was performing a ritual, dancing and chanting to the muffled beat of a small drum. The man was masked, and carried a small doll-like figure, decorated with paint and feathers. He could see quite plainly despite the dim light. He watched a tiny bit of fluff from one of the breath-feathers that adorned the doll, as it broke free and floated in the air near the fire. He could even see the reddened area from the bleeding of the prostrate man's chest wound. There was only mild curiosity as to the identity of the man on the mat. That individual lay dying, it appeared, but dying seemed of no special importance.

He looked above him, and found that he was near the poles that formed support for a roof. He seemed to be suspended there somehow . . . no, not suspended, there were no ropes or cords. He was hovering, as an eagle hovers on barely fluttering wings, watching the scene below. He concentrated again on the figures there. Besides the medicine man, and the other medicine man who beat the drum, there was another who sat to one side, and one other who knelt near the unconscious figure, concern showing on his face, the worry apparent.

There was something familiar about this man, though all the others seemed to be strangers. Except, of course, the man on the mat. He now identified that figure as his own, and the other, who waited with quiet concern, was Woodchuck, his father. But how could this be? Yes, the man who lay dying on the floor in this ceremonial lodge of some other tribe was plainly Red Feather, young man of the People. But how could he also hover near the roof and watch himself die? It was a matter of no great concern, except that it was a curious experience. There was no pain, but a calm detachment that let him feel sorrow for his father's loss. He wished that he could reassure his father that it would be nothing to worry over. His spirit had already crossed over, and the medicine man had no need to sing the chants and make medicine to heal the prostrate body.

No sooner had he realized that this was a thing of the spirit, however, than he was aware of other spirits around him. There was a wordless communication, a contact that he did not have, had never had, with the living persons below. He almost felt pity for those trapped in bodies of flesh, which dulled and distorted the understanding that he now had as a free spirit.

The other spirits were hovering, floating, around him, interested observers. One, who seemed a person with authority, kept attempting to persuade him to return to his body. Oddly, the wraith-like form greatly resembled that of the medicine-doll in the hand of the dancer below. Red Feather felt no need to go back, did not want to go, and resented a bit this effort to make him do so. The chanting was rising to a frantic climax, and the drum quickened.

It was at that moment that he became aware of a shadowy spirit-figure near him, the figure of a woman, young and beautiful. He could see her quite plainly, the tenderness in her face. With the wordless communication of the Spirit World, he knew that this was his mother. Not Yellow Head, who had raised him, but his own mother, Pink Cloud, who had been killed during his infancy.

"Mother?" he questioned.

"Yes, little one, my little Ground Squirrel," she smiled at him.

Ground Squirrel. The pet name that had stuck, that he had grown up wearing, not Red Feather, the proud name of his grandfather. Well, no matter.

"I have come to you," he said.

"No, no, it is not time for you. You must go back."

"But I want . . ."

The thought was left unfinished. He felt himself being drawn downward, pulled back toward his body, as if by a rope. He wanted to fight it, to remain in the Spirit World, but it was beyond his control. He was being drawn by the powerful medicine of the dancer, the medicine-doll, and the spirit he had encountered who looked like . . .

There was a sort of click, as he reentered his body. Pain washed over him in a wave, and a desperate need for air to breathe. His chest was one massive ache, and each motion to draw air in and out resulted in another spasm.

The drum stopped and the medicine man slumped, exhausted. He spoke a few words to the man with the drum, who answered.

Red Feather did not understand, as they spoke in a tongue unfamiliar to him. His father came over and knelt beside him.

"You have come back to us," Woodchuck spoke softly.

The young medicine man looked at him and spoke words he did not understand. Red Feather was certain that he should know this man, but it was such an effort to think. The whole thing was more confusing, even, than his short journey to the Spirit World and back. What had happened? How was he injured?

"You rest now," his father was saying.

Red Feather closed his eyes. He *must* think a little before he slept. He would go back, to before they reached Santa Fe. That must be when it all began . . .

# 2

>> >> >>

**G**round Squirrel's horse topped the rise, and he reined the animal aside so he could pause to appreciate the view. Ahead of him, the others were stopping, too. The pack horses, sensing a rest stop, began to wander along the shoulder of the hill, browsing on the sparse growth that clung there.

Behind him Sky-Eyes, bringing up the rear of the little caravan, paused long enough to study the back trail a few moments. Then he kneed his mount over beside that of Ground Squirrel.

"Well, what do you think?" he asked with a smile.

The young man sat speechless, not knowing how to answer. In all his sixteen summers, there had never been an experience like this journey. Since his childhood, the People had been trading in Santa Fe. Each summer, a pack train carrying furs and robes would wend its way from the tallgrass plains to the eastern slopes of the mountains, then follow the ancient Southwest Trail to the settlements of the Spanish Hairfaces. There, they would trade for weapons and tools of steel, and other useful things. He could well remember the excitement that had accompanied the first expedition. The area was relatively unknown, and it was considered a dangerous project.

His father, Woodchuck, waved from where his horse stood at the head of the column, and Ground Squirrel waved back. It was a great honor to be allowed to accompany the trading party this year. Usually either his father or Sky-Eyes, or both, led the expedition. Sometimes one or both of the wives had gone along. He had often heard the story of how Pale Star, with her experience in trading, had helped to make that first expedition a success. She had been a captive as a child, he had heard, owned by a traveling trader, and had developed the skills. His father and Star's husband, Sky-Eyes, had possessed some knowledge of the Spanish, and spoke their tongue. Squirrel was not quite certain about that part of it. The two men had originally been outsiders. Hairfaces, in fact, though not like the Spanish. Another tribe, it seemed. They thought nothing of dealing with other tribes, as it had been the way of their upbringing. Now, both were men of the People, well-respected family men, prominent in the tribe.

The trade had benefited the People enormously. More than anything since the coming of the horse, some of the elders said. Though it was hard to imagine, that in itself had been only a few generations ago. The elk-dog had allowed easier hunting of the buffalo, and brought an end to winter's Moon of Starvation. Ground Squirrel had heard the story all his life, seen it reenacted in song and dance.

But the importance of the trading was that of metal tools. Until then, the People had only stone tools, except for a knife or two brought by his father and Sky-Eyes when they joined the People. Now, every family had steel knives, lance points, and arrowheads. These had been regarded almost with reverence at first. "Medicine knives," they were called, acknowledging their strength and power.

Already, the medicine had become commonplace, as the steel instruments came into everyday use. The People benefited greatly from further trading with other tribes to the east and north, for other items of value. The People were respected widely, not only for their skill with the horse, but for their expertise in trading.

This was the first season that Ground Squirrel had been allowed to accompany the pack train, and he was proud. He had been a quick student in the skills of the Rabbit Society. He could shoot, ride, run, and swim well, and had killed his first buffalo in the fall hunt, using the lance. It was a great honor, then, when Sky-Eyes had suggested to his father that he be allowed to go along. This would increase his credibility as a man of the People when the time came to take a wife. He had not yet found a girl who impressed him as one who could fulfill that responsibility, but no matter. He had not yet undertaken his vision-quest. It would be better to do that first, before establishing their lodge anyway, he supposed.

Part of the problem with finding a wife, although he probably did not realize it at the time, was the very competence of the women in his life. His stepmother, Yellow Head, had been widowed and captured, along with her daughter, by a tribe to the east. They had escaped and were making their way home when they encountered Woodchuck, also returning to his wife's people. Ground Squirrel's own mother had been killed in an accident when he was an infant, and he had no memory of her. Yellow Head had been a strong mother to him.

The other woman close to his family was Pale Star. In addition to her trading skills, Star was fluent in several languages, and was one of the tribe's best storytellers. He had seen her hold an audience spellbound with her rendition of the Creation Story of the People, or of Long-ago Times when the animals talked, or of his favorite stories of all, those of the Old Man of the Shadows.

It was little wonder, perhaps, that the young man had not found a woman who measured up to the ideal seen in these women. Even Sunflower, his stepsister, a few years older than he, was a strong woman. Sunflower was married now, with a lodge of her own.

In all probability, it would take a woman the stature of the legendary warrior-woman Running Eagle to attract the attention of Ground Squirrel. He did not realize this as a problem, of course. His attention was elsewhere. He was completely distracted by the expedition and its goals.

He could not even visualize a village of several hundred people, maybe more, living in permanent mud-brick lodges. *Aiee,* how could one catch the cool night breeze without lifting the edge of the lodge-skin to open the dwelling to the night? He was eager to see how this was done.

Just now, however, his attention was focused on the broad panorama before him. This crest, Sky-Eyes had told him, was called Raton Pass by the Spanish. From here, it was mostly downhill to the city they sought. But the view here . . . it was magnificent. They were looking south, and the plain stretched before them to earth's rim. To the east, a distant range of mountains stretched south into the dim blue distance. It was much like standing on a high point in the Sacred Hills of the People, and looking as far as eye could see. Different, though. This was higher, overlooking a wider expanse of plains. The main difference, though, was the color. In the Sacred Hills, the summer colors were greens, the green of the prairie grasses and the darker green of the trees along the streams. In the distance, each ridge became more bluish, until finally there would be no difference in the shade of the hills and the blue of the sky where they met.

Here, there were reds and yellows and the gray-green of sparse vegetation. Colors in the distance became more purple. *Aiee,* this was a strange land. He could feel its spirit reach out to him, offering the hint of mystery, danger, and romance.

His father reined past the browsing pack animals and rode back to join them.

"It is beautiful, no?" he asked.

"Yes," agreed Ground Squirrel. "It is a strange spirit." Woodchuck and Sky-Eyes laughed.

"Yes, a strange spirit," Woodchuck agreed. "Not like our country, or the mountains, but a spirit of its own."

"Is it so in Santa Fe?"

"Some, maybe. That is a spirit of its own, too. At the edge of the mountains. Never mind, you will see."

"We will be there soon?"

"Soon? Well, several sleeps, before we get there. We will stop at another town, first."

"A Hairface town?"

"No, no, not Spanish. Mud-lodge people. They are our friends. We stay at their town when we pass this way."

"In their lodges?" Ground Squirrel asked in alarm.

His was the typical fear felt by people of the plains, the fear of an enclosure. All his life, Ground Squirrel had lived in a skin lodge, moved from place to place as they followed the seasons and the buffalo, or met with the other bands for the annual Sun Dance and the Big Council. In summer, the lodge cover was lifted and adjusted to allow the fresh breezes to cool their dwelling. In winter, the lower edge was pegged tightly to the ground, and packed with dry grasses inside the lining to protect from winter storms. It was difficult for him to visualize the permanent dwellings of the mud-lodge people.

Perhaps, he thought, they are like the lodges of the Growers. In his own prairie country, the People often traded with the Growers who lived along the streams. Robes and meat were exchanged for corn, beans, and pumpkins. The People traditionally thought of Growers as unable or unwilling to hunt. This did not in any way lessen the value of trading with them. It was simply a different way of life, one considered inferior to the hunting of buffalo in the wide-open sweep of the plains.

Ground Squirrel had once been inside a Grower dwelling. The People were camped nearby to trade, and the children were becoming acquainted, there being no language barrier among the young. He was playing with a boy about his own age, some seven summers, and had accompanied his new friend to his lodge.

They were completely inside the dwelling, dug partially into the ground and built of logs and mud, before the panic struck. There was no way out except the door, he realized. The animal smell of human habitation rushed at him, a smothering, frightening thing, and Ground Squirrel turned and fled, from the lodge and even the village. He did not stop until he was in the open, drawing in deep lungfuls of clean prairie air.

His reminiscence was interrupted now. It was time to move on. The others were rounding up the straying pack horses, to follow Woodchuck's lead down the trail toward the south. Ground Squirrel's spirits were high. He was entering new country, a time of new experiences and excitement. He could hardly wait to see what lay ahead. This was the greatest adventure of his life, and his heart felt good about it.

# 3

>> >> >>

The pack train threaded its way on down the mountain. Sky-Eyes and Woodchuck were pleased with this season's packs, Ground Squirrel knew. Eight pack horses, heavily laden. Five were from their own tribe, the other three belonging to one of their allies. Lean Bear and Turkey Foot, of the Head Splitters, represented that tribe's interest in the trading venture. Both had been on the original expedition years before, and had remained close friends of Sky-Eyes ever since. They, too, spoke of the quality of this year's pelts.

It had been a good winter for trapping, cold enough to make the fur thick and soft, yet open enough to allow easy travel. They had many pelts of beaver, otter, fox, and mink, as well as soft-tanned buffalo robes. They should be able to exchange for good quantities of tools and weapons and iron to make arrow points, Sky-Eyes said. Already, a man or two of the People had learned to work with the spirit of the hot iron, hammering it while soft into a shape to use. Ground Squirrel had watched this procedure, carried out by a man of the Northern Band, at the time of the Big Council. It was said that one of the Head Splitters, too, was skilled in this medicine.

His interests, however, were along less practical lines. His desire was to experience the sights and sounds, the tastes and smells, of Santa Fe, and the mixture of customs found there. During the years of his growing up, he had heard tales each season when the trading party returned. Tales of exotic foods, of strange customs. There were birds, for instance, kept and raised for eating, like dogs, it was said. Other animals, too. One, he had heard, grew fur that could be removed without removing the skin. He would have doubted this story, except that his father had brought to Yellow Head one year a robe which he said was made of this fur. And, wonder of wonders, the robe was of fur on both sides, without a skin! It was tightly twisted and woven together much like the baskets that some of the tribes made of grasses and other materials.

His father also told of a sort of carrier, like a pole-drag, but rolling on two short pieces of log. Woodchuck tried to describe it, but it was beyond the comprehension of young Ground Squirrel. And now, he was to be able to see for himself. He did not think he could even sleep until they arrived at their destination, and he began to experience these things of wonder. What strong medicine these Spanish must have, he thought. All of the marvelous medicine-things, the knives, woven fur blankets and *serapes*, and their various domestic animals.

He remembered the retelling of the story of Heads Off and the First Elk-dog. An outsider who had become one of the People long ago, Heads Off had been riding the first horse ever seen by the People. In the course of a few years, and many horses, Heads Off had become a sub-chief. Even now, his Elk-dog Medicine, the bit with the iron ring, was in the possession of Looks Far, the medicine man. It had been handed down through the generations, and was highly revered as a symbol of the medicine that enabled control of the horse.

Now, it had been learned, there were many of the medicine-bits, in common use by the Spanish. Sky-Eyes had once told him that he was sure Heads Off must have been a Spaniard, partly because of the medicine-bit. It would have been many seasons ago, Sky-Eyes and Woodchuck believed. There were several generations in the memory of people now living, and the time of Heads Off was before that. The People were not accustomed to accurately recording the passage of time. Events were either recent or "a long time ago."

Still, it was remembered that Pale Star was a granddaughter of the great warrior-woman Running Eagle. She, in turn, was a daughter of Eagle, who had been a son or grandson of Heads Off. At that point, the elders of the People would spread their hands in perplexity.

"I do not know, Sky-Eyes. Does it matter? That was a long time ago."

Ground Squirrel had asked about the name, "Heads Off." No one knew the reason for the name, it seemed. That part of the story had been lost. Sky-Eyes thought it may have related to the round metal headdresses used by the Spanish. To one who had never seen this equipment, a person taking off such headgear might appear to be removing his own head. Ground Squirrel did not quite understand.

"No matter. You will see what they look like," Woodchuck told him.

They spent one night camped near a mud-brick town, with lodges piled high on top of each other. The travelers were guests of one of the chiefs who was called Blue Corn, a friend of long standing. Ground Squirrel even managed to overcome his fear of enclosures to some extent, and was interested in the new foods served them.

Not a little of his interest, perhaps, was stimulated by the beauty of a dark-eyed young woman of about his own age. She seemed constantly at his side, serving him with the choicest of morsels when opportunity offered. Her eyes were large and well spaced, with long lashes and an expressive depth that reminded him of deep pools in the clear prairie streams of home. Her smile was shy, but friendly, and he longed to talk with her. Her name, he learned through his father's interpretation, was Moonflower. She spoke none of the tongue of the People, but some Spanish. This, of course, was of no use to Ground Squirrel, who had very little knowledge of Spanish. He tried sign talk. The sign talk was not normally used by these mud-lodge people, his father said, but some, like this village in intermittent contact with the people of the plains, had begun to use it some.

He was delighted to find that Moonflower understood a few signs. After the meal was finished, and while the old friends visited, the two young people attempted to carry on a conversation. There was probably more laughter and fun than understanding, but it did not seem to matter. He did learn that Blue Corn, the girl's father, was one of the "Elder Brothers," a group of chiefs whose authority was greatly respected. There seemed to be no head chief, as in his own tribe.

When they departed next morning, Ground Squirrel had some regrets. Moonflower watched them go, a wave of the hand and a shy smile impressing him greatly.

"I will come back!" he signed.

The girl nodded in understanding.

They were nearing Santa Fe when they encountered the Spanish patrol. Ground Squirrel had never seen a military unit before, and was astonished by their uniforms, the sameness of every warrior.

"They are all alike!" he marveled.

Sky-Eyes chuckled.

"Yes, it is made to be so."

The nearest thing to this in the experience of the boy was seen in the ceremonial dress of the warrior societies. The Blood Society, especially, their headdresses and leggings all alike, had always been an exciting group in the ceremonials. Their symbolic face paint, the crimson band across the forehead, with another across each cheek, their robes and leggings, all alike, had captured many a boyish imagination.

But Ground Squirrel had seen nothing like this. The lancers, some twelve in number, were dressed precisely alike, white sashes crossed over bright-colored tunics. Only the leader wore the round metal headdress, he saw. The other soldiers wore a sort of cap, of material and color to match the tunics. Perhaps most impressive of all, their weapons were all the same. Except for the chief and one other who seemed a sort of sub-chief, each warrior carried a long lance. The steel points sparkled in the sun,

and colorful streamers fluttered from just below, like eagle feathers on the shaft of a ceremonial spear of the
People. His heart beat wildly with the thrill of excitement.

Now the patrol was approaching. The chief with the
metal headdress kneed his horse forward, and with the
sub-chief beside him, rode slowly to where the pack train
had halted. The rest of the soldiers waited, perhaps
twenty paces away. Ground Squirrel saw that the two
chiefs, who did not carry lances, were armed with long
knives which hung at their waists. Knives as long as his
arm, the young man noted with a shudder. *Aiee,* what
damage such a weapon could inflict in combat!

Of course, there had been little combat in his lifetime.
Since the People and their traditional enemies, the Head
Splitters, had become allies, in fact. That was in the
memory of people now living. The two tribes had banded
together to face a common enemy, an invader from the
north. The enemy had been driven out, and now the only
combat was an occasional skirmish with some of the
tribes of the forests to the east.

Now Sky-Eyes gave the familiar sign, right hand raised
with palm forward, to show peaceful intent. The soldiers
casually returned the gesture, and they began to talk.
Ground Squirrel, who knew only the tongue of the People, and enough Head Splitter words to get along, was
extremely frustrated. He wished they would use hand-
sign talk so that he could follow the conversation. Then
he remembered, his father had said that the Spanish use
hand-sign very little. *Aiee,* how could a tribe whose medicine was so strong be so backward in this respect, he
wondered.

Well, he saw now that it would be to his advantage to
learn the tongue of the Spanish. Necessary, almost, if he
followed the custom of trading, like his father and Sky-
Eyes.

# 4

>> >> >>

"*Buenos días, amigos,*" smiled Sergeant Villa. "It is good to see you again."

Villa was no different from year to year, Sky-Eyes noted to himself. A trifle more grizzled, perhaps, but ageless. The leathery old sergeant, the professional soldier on whose shoulders falls the day-to-day responsibility of running an army. Young, inexperienced officers, fresh out of training, might come and go. Some would become successful, while some failed. Those who succeeded would do so because they were able to learn from some experienced old sergeant in one of their first commands. He well remembered the sergeant who had taught him, in a time and place worlds away. He had been Lieutenant André Du Pres then, of His Majesty's service, an existence he seldom recalled now.

He had also learned much from a capable young sergeant whose feel for the spirit of the new world had been uncanny. Jean Cartier was the man's name, and they had become fast friends, closer than brothers. He glanced to his right to see if Woodchuck, once Jean Cartier, was feeling the same things. He could not tell.

The reason for such nostalgia at this moment was that Villa seemed to be breaking in a new lieutenant. The officer who sat beside him was quite young and officious. The look on his face was arrogant, almost insolent, in the

16

security of his newly assigned authority. Sky-Eyes was amused.

"Good day, Señor," he said politely. "I am Sky-Eyes, of the Elk-dog People. We come to trade."

"This is Lieutenant Gomez," explained Sergeant Villa. "Lieutenant Diaz is captain now."

"That will do, Sergeant," snapped Gomez crisply. "What do you people have to trade?"

Ah, thought Sky-Eyes, a real martinet. Villa has his hands full with this one. It was time for the next move, the cross-the-palm-with-silver, native style. He rummaged in a small pack, tied behind his saddle for convenience, and drew out a prime otter skin, which he handed to the lieutenant.

"Goods such as this, Lieutenant. I am pleased to present this as a gift."

The officer relaxed a trifle, obviously impressed. He stroked the soft fur.

"Yes, I see. You have been here before, I take it?"

"Yes, Señor. That is how we know the Sergeant Villa."

"They have come for many years, Lieutenant. They are friends of Captain Diaz," interjected Villa.

"I see."

His manner became a bit more respectful, though his basic distrust of natives was still plain. He turned to the sergeant.

"Dismount the platoon. We will take a rest stop."

Villa turned and barked the command, and the lancers dismounted to relax and stretch saddle-weary bodies. The members of the trading party also dismounted, allowing the horses to graze. Lieutenant Gomez asked a few superficial questions and then drew aside, as if it was beneath his dignity to associate with natives. Villa was eager to talk, as soon as the officer was out of earshot.

"Captain Martinez went back to Spain," he began. "Diaz is in his job."

"There is a change in administration?" asked Woodchuck.

"No, not much. No trouble, anyway. Just the usual shuffle. It was time for Martinez to go home."

"Is Diaz pleased?"

"Of course. He misses the patrols, but he likes the assignment."

"And your new officer?" Sky-Eyes asked.

"Straight from the Academy," sighed Villa. "I think he will work out, but he has much to learn. I am glad Diaz is above him."

"And Gutierrez, the trader?"

"Ah, yes. Enrico. He is the same. No better, no worse," Villa smiled. "He asked about you only last week."

The others smiled. They had traded through all the years with Enrico Gutierrez. He made a big point of being a sharp trader, and enjoyed the harangue, the give and take of the bargaining. Sky-Eyes loved to watch Gutierrez and Pale Star in a trading session. Both were experts, and each recognized the skills of the other. With all of this, however, the trader had always treated them fairly. He had made suggestions from time to time, as to what commodities might trade well. They had tried dried meat, which was not too successful, since fresh meat was available. Pemmican, dried meat mixed with melted fat and berries and stored in intestines like sausages, was a more acceptable commodity. However, the heat of the long pack trip made pemmican a little questionable. Gutierrez had developed a taste for it, and they usually tried to bring some as a personal favor, but as a trading commodity it had not worked out well. Furs and a few robes made the bulk of the commerce.

It was understood that Gutierrez had always paid a percentage of his profit to Diaz and Martinez, with a smaller thank offering to the sergeant. This procedure oiled the wheels of commerce, and guaranteed protection for the pack train while in their sphere of influence. Most important, it avoided the endless formalities and regulations that could easily be imposed if the traders incurred the ill will of the military authorities.

Sky-Eyes wondered whether the new lieutenant, Gomez, would be included in the arrangement. He apparently had not been informed thus far. It would probably be necessary for Diaz, now Captain Diaz, to continue the custom, however. If Gomez ever decided that he was being excluded from such a payoff, he could make trouble on up the chain of command. Ah, well, that was not their concern. It amused Sky-Eyes that he had once anticipated a career in just such a political quagmire.

He wondered if Diaz would inform the new man of their French background. Both Diaz and Martinez had been aware of it, though he thought Sergeant Villa had not. It had seemed less important as the years passed. Sky-Eyes and Woodchuck had both adopted the dress and hairstyle of the People. Except for the blue eyes that gave him his name, there was nothing to betray that part of their past. They had been accepted as native traders from the plains.

"Who is the young man?" Villa asked.

"Oh, this is my son, Ground Squirrel," Woodchuck answered quickly.

"Ah, yes, Ground Squirrel, a little Woodchuck," acknowledged Villa.

The family resemblance between father and son was a joke among the People. Cartier's prominent front teeth, and especially his round cheeks, had earned him the name "Woodchuck." When his infant son showed the same cheeky visage, he had immediately been dubbed Ground Squirrel and the name had stuck. This, despite the fact that he had been named Red Feather after his grandfather, chief of the Eastern Band. It was a small source of irritation to the young man.

"I was explaining who you are," Woodchuck told his son, in the People's tongue.

"And about the little Woodchuck, I suppose," the boy said resignedly.

"No, he guessed that part," smiled Woodchuck. "You cannot avoid it. But this man is an old friend, my son. Sergeant Villa."

"What means his name?"

"His name? Well, a sergeant is a sort of sub-chief. It would be like calling him Chief Villa."

"And the other part?"

"Well, 'villa' is a word for 'lodge' in their tongue. But, often their names seem to mean nothing, as ours do."

"*Aiee!* Names that mean nothing?"

"Yes. Only names."

"They have strange ways, these people," Ground Squirrel noted.

"That is true. But they think ours strange."

Lieutenant Gomez now rose and called to the sergeant. The rest stop was over. Lean Bear was rounding up the horses and leading the way out on the trail, the pack horses following his horse by long-ingrained habit. Sky-Eyes moved to take the rear, and Woodchuck and his son fell in behind him.

"We will see you in a day or two," called Villa, "when we come back from patrol."

Lieutenant Gomez sat stiffly in the saddle without turning as he led the platoon away. There, thought Sky-Eyes, is a strange one. I wonder what makes him so.

# 5
## >> >> >>

The square in Santa Fe had changed very little since last season. Not since they had started trading there, actually. The long low government building sat solidly, brooding behind its overhanging promenade. Its massive timbers were unchanged, and a new whitewash on the walls reflected the afternoon sunlight.

The traders stopped in the thin shade of the trees in the plaza, and dismounted. Sky-Eyes and Woodchuck started toward a small door near one end of the building.

"Come on, Squirrel," his father called. "Lean Bear will watch the horses."

The young man hastened to catch up.

"This is where we trade?" he asked, in awe of the gigantic building, the largest structure he had ever seen.

"No, no," Woodchuck answered. "We only stop here to pay our respects to the Diaz-chief."

"This is his lodge?"

"No. This is . . . *aiee*, son, you . . . look, this is like a council lodge, as some tribes have."

"I see. Is this Diaz their band chief?"

"No, he is like a sub-chief, but greater than the one we saw on the trail. This one is leader of this warrior society."

Woodchuck relaxed a little, pleased with his ability to translate the situation into understandable terms. The three stepped up on the wooden floor and nodded to the armed sentry who marched slowly up and down under the overhang of the promenade. The soldier nodded in return, quite familiar with this party through their years of trading.

Lieutenant, now Captain, Diaz rose with a smile from behind his desk, as they entered his inner office.

"Ah, welcome, *mis amigos!* It is good to see you again."

"Yes, it is good," Sky-Eyes agreed, clasping the extended hand. "You have risen in the world!"

"It comes eventually," laughed the officer.

He shook the hand of Woodchuck and turned to the young man with a smile.

"This, I presume, will be the young Woodchuck!"

"Yes, señor, but he is a little tired of that joke," Woodchuck smiled. "He has a name . . . Red Feather, after his grandfather, a great chief. I should probably use it more."

Diaz laughed.

"I understand. Welcome, Red Feather, son of my friend."

He held out his hand.

"Does the boy speak Spanish?"

All conversation had been in Spanish.

"No. Only a little. Another error in his upbringing. But, he has grown up so fast!"

The three men laughed, and Ground Squirrel looked uncomfortable.

"I have just told him you are my son, Red Feather, who will be wanting to learn Spanish," Woodchuck explained to the boy in the tongue of the People. "He has welcomed you as a friend."

"Not 'Little Woodchuck'?"

"No," said Woodchuck seriously, "Red Feather."

"Thank you, Father," murmured the boy, pleased. "Please tell him that I am happy to be here, as his friend."

Woodchuck relayed the information, and Diaz nodded.

"Is there much change with your promotion?" Sky-Eyes asked.

THE FLOWER IN THE MOUNTAINS >> 23

THE FLOWER IN THE MOUNTAINS >> 23

Sergeant Villa had given his opinion, but that of the unit's commander might well be different.

"I think not," Diaz grinned. "I have been here long enough to know the chain of command."

"We still deal with Gutierrez, I take it?"

"Yes, of course. You spoke with Sergeant Villa?"

"Yes. We saw him yesterday. What of the lieutenant, Gomez?"

"A strange one, is he not?" chuckled Diaz. "A hard worker, ambitious. This reminds me, I have not spoken to him of your special status."

"You mean as French?"

"No, no, your status as preferred traders. I will explain to him when they return. A day or two."

"It is good. But, now, it grows late. We should take our furs to Gutierrez before dark."

"Yes, of course. I will look for you later. Shall we share a glass of wine?"

"Certainly. After we camp. Back here?"

"Yes, good. I will expect you both . . . all three. Who else is with you?"

"Lean Bear, Turkey Foot."

"Neither of your wives? I am disappointed! You will give my regards to your charming ladies, of course?"

Diaz was gallant, as always. The three left the building and rejoined the others in the plaza. The shadows were growing longer as they remounted and headed down one of the narrow streets toward Gutierrez's trading post.

Lean Bear kneed his horse over to ride beside Woodchuck.

"Someone was looking for you," he said casually.

"For me? Who was it?"

"I do not know, Woodchuck. I never saw this man before."

"What did he want?"

"He did not say. He asked you to meet him tonight, after dark."

"I do not understand."

"Nor do I, Woodchuck. But he gave me this to give you."

Lean Bear handed Woodchuck a medicine stick, with an eagle's head carved at one end. He examined it critically.

"Yes, this is one I carved."

Woodchuck was well known among the People and among the Head Splitters, too, for his skill with a knife. He had carved, over the years, hundreds of small wooden toys and medicine objects, such as this. Usually he gave them away, though he had traded some to other tribes for various necessities. This medicine stick was old, most likely one of his earliest efforts. He racked his brain, but could not recall the circumstances of its creation. It must have been traded for something he needed, or else given to a special person. It was no ordinary gift.

"What did this man look like?" he asked Lean Bear.

"Like nothing, Woodchuck. Just a man."

"A Hairface? Blue eyes? What about him? How was he dressed?"

"Oh. No, not a Hairface. From some other tribe, one I do not know. Different manner of hair, different cut to his buckskins."

Now Woodchuck was completely confused. Who could possibly want to see him, and why all the secrecy?

"Where am I to meet him?"

"He said he will find you."

Woodchuck felt the hairs prickle at the back of his neck. It was uncomfortable, not knowing. Was this mysterious man some old enemy, seeking revenge? If so, what was he doing with a medicine stick carved by Woodchuck? The uneasy thought crossed his mind that an enemy might have gained possession of the stick and be using it to work some sort of medicine-spell. He could think of no enemies who might wish to do him harm. He had had few enemies in his life, much preferring to relate easily and amiably to all those he encountered. The last one who could really be called an enemy was a relative of Yellow Head's captor, long before their meeting. It had been necessary to kill that one, who had tried to wreak vengeance. Surely, after all these years, not another, looking for vengeance.

No, that could not be it, he decided. If such a thing was happening, the man, whoever he might be, would never have given up the medicine stick.

This led to other questions. Why would someone give up possession of such a fetish, except to accomplish something very important? Or possibly in the sure knowledge that it would be returned. Yes, that must be the secret. This was not an enemy, but a friend. A good friend, apparently, who would be certain of the return of his medicine stick.

But this raised yet another question. If this was such a simple and straightforward thing, why all the secrecy? Why had the man not waited for him in the square, to renew old friendships?

# 6
>> >> >>

Woodchuck sat listening to the night sounds, trying to sort out the puzzle of the medicine stick. When the party made camp, he had volunteered as lookout for the first watch, so that he could be alone to think.

Gutierrez had welcomed them warmly, and had assisted in unloading the packs and carrying them inside for the night. The trading would take place in the morning, but it was much easier to relax for the night, resting in the knowledge that their furs were safe in the trader's warehouse. They had returned to spend a convivial evening with Captain Diaz, and were now settled in for the night.

They had always camped at this place, a traditional campground because of its location, fuel, water, and grass for the horses. In recent years grass was not so available. Santa Fe was growing, and there was more traffic, more trading in the area. The pack animals and riding animals devoured more of the grass. Someday it would be necessary to camp farther from the sprawling town, but just now this was sufficient. It was certainly better than staying in town. Woodchuck, in the years since he became a man of the People, had come to feel things as they did. Although he had been raised among houses and buildings, now they seemed foreign to him. The structures seemed like traps, after life in skin lodges, and he was glad to be able to camp outside of the town. Sky-Eyes had admitted that he felt the same.

Just now, however, Woodchuck was thinking of other things. He had said nothing to Sky-Eyes or Ground Squirrel about the carved stick, largely because he had nothing to say. Perhaps after he knew more, there would be something to tell. He had still not come to any conclusion about the meaning of the strange occurrence, but it had stirred his memory. He was probing back into his past, trying to remember when he started carving the small toys and fetishes. It had started with willow whistles for the children, then animals and birds. When it became apparent that the carved creatures were regarded as important medicine, he began to refine them. Many warriors of the People carried the fetishes of Woodchuck with great pride, drawing strength from their medicine.

There had been a time when he stopped carving and whittling completely for a year, after the death of Pink Cloud, Squirrel's mother. He had returned to the civilization of the outpost at Fort Mishi-ghan, but it was useless. It had taken several years, but he overcame his grief and returned to the People. Meanwhile, he had begun to whittle out of boredom. Gradually, he developed the interest and the skills again.

It was that part of his past which kept returning to him now, in some strange and forgotten way which he could not quite define. This medicine stick, which he now held in his clenched palm, seemed to belong to that time period, before he rejoined the People. Possibly, even, the journey back. He had carved as he traveled, out of boredom and impatience, but . . . no, that was not it. Something was missing, eluding his memory.

He sighed deeply, and gazed up at the stars. The new moon had set shortly after dark, and the sky was like black velvet, studded with a myriad of sparkling lights. The camp fires of the Spirit World, some called them fancifully. He watched the Seven Hunters, wheeling their precise arc around the Real-star. It was a beautiful night, with just a touch of a chill in the mountain air. He shifted his back comfortably against a sun-warmed boul-

der. He had taken this position, low and with his back
protected, so as not to be seen as he watched. Sentries
had been shot or struck down many times because of a
visible silhouette against the night sky. Woodchuck was a
soldier, and a good one, whether a soldier in His Majesty's service, or in a warrior society of the People. The fact
that he was still alive attested to his skill.

A night bird called, the mysterious creature with the
hollow cry. The "Pierre-bird" they had called it, among
the French troops. Its mournful call sounded much like
some supernatural being, crying over and over, the same
despairing question, as to the whereabouts of the lost
Pierre: *"Pour Pierre?"*

The sound of the creature and its hopeless despair
made him think again of his return to the People. He had
traveled through a heavily wooded region west of the
Great River, the Father of Waters, and there had been
many such birds there.

Another Pierre-bird now answered, closer at hand, or
maybe it was the same one, moving from one tree to another. They must have difficulty, in a land with few
trees . . . He stopped the thought suddenly, and laid his
hand carefully on his belt-ax, while he tried to remember. Were there any Pierre-birds here in the mountains?
He was not certain, but it seemed that it was not right.
The night crier seemed more suited to the heavy, damp
regions of the forests along the Great River.

But he was also remembering that this cry was often
used as a signal by the tribes of the woodlands. Was this a
bird, or a warrior, hiding in the darkness, signaling to
others?

There was silence now, which made him all the more
suspicious. The Pierre-birds would often call for hours,
he recalled, from the same position. If the caller out there
in the darkness was a man, it would explain the fact that
no two calls had come from the same area. Now he was
certain that the mouth that had shaped those hollow
tones was human, and his neck hairs prickled nervously.
He was also certain now that, whatever the mystery of
the night caller, it was connected to the other, the medi-

cine stick. These odd occurrences seemed to relate to him, to Woodchuck, for reasons he could not explain, and it worried him.

There had been silence for some time now. There was, among the night sounds, no cry that sounded remotely like that of the Pierre-bird. Experimentally, Woodchuck cupped his hands around his mouth and gave a tentative cry.

*"Pour Pierre?"*

Almost instantly his call was answered, from close at hand. So close, in fact, that he jumped in surprise. He sat waiting, grasping his ax with sweating palms, unsure what his next move would be. He had to be ready to defend himself, yet had no idea against what, or from which direction. Despite this, there were some indications that the person out there might be a friend. An enemy would have had opportunity to kill him already.

Maybe his adversary was only playing with him. The man out there in the dark knew all about his quarry, while Woodchuck knew nothing. He felt like an aging buffalo bull, waiting for the certainty of the circling wolves. No, more like the helpless half-grown rabbit he had once seen captured by a fox. The vixen was careful to keep it alive, carrying it to her pups as part of their training. The youngsters had played with the hapless creature for some time, repeatedly allowing it to almost escape, only to drag it down again. He had been able to watch with a detached interest, knowing that this was the way of all things, some living things preying on others to survive.

Now such a contest had taken on a very personal meaning. He had the feeling that the stalker out there was playing with him. His flesh crawled with the uncertainty of the thing. He had no fear of a direct attack, but this unknown something out there was disturbing. He wanted to break and run, but knew that would be the worst possible move. Instead, he tried to gather his muscles to spring when the time came. He was in an awkward position, his feet not properly under him as he sat. Now there was something moving out in front of him. Something he felt, rather than saw or heard. The suspense was becoming unbearable.

"Woodchuck?" came a soft whisper. "Is it you?"

His head whirled. The voice was unfamiliar, but there were other things. The stalker knew his name, which was not surprising, but was a little unsure of himself. Woodchuck felt more confident. This was no supernatural being with boundless knowledge, but a man, with certain doubts and fears of his own. Woodchuck was so relieved that it took a moment for him to realize another fact that did not fit. The soft call from the darkness had been in *French.*

Of the people in his life at the present time, only Sky-Eyes and Pale Star were fluent in French. He supposed that some of the Spanish at Santa Fe knew French as a second language, but it was not generally spoken. Besides, he had a strong feeling that this was not a Spaniard. The entire scene was out of character.

"Yes?" he answered cautiously with his own question.

Thinking rapidly meanwhile, he arrived at a conclusion. This must be a native, to use the birdcall in communicating with him. One who spoke French, so from his distant past. But why . . . A dim shape moved toward him, slowly and without threatening motion. The man sank to a sitting position, not an arm's length from him. Woodchuck gripped his ax, still tense.

"It has been a long time, my friend," the other man said.

"Who are you?" Woodchuck blurted.

"I thought you knew! You answered my call. I am Pretty Weasel."

Pretty Weasel. Of course. It came rushing back to him now. He and Pretty Weasel, of one of the Eastern tribes, had been guiding a French exploring party down the Great River. Woodchuck, homesick for his son and the People, had abandoned the party, leaving them to be guided by Weasel. But what was the man doing here in the West, and why in God's name was he being so secretive?

"You found your people?" Weasel was asking. It was more a statement than a question.

"Yes, of course. Weasel, what are you doing here? And why all the mystery? Here, your medicine stick."

He handed the object to the other man. He remembered now, he had given it to Pretty Weasel on the night he had left the exploring party. Weasel tucked it in his medicine pouch.

"I thought that might tell you who I was. That and the night bird's call."

Woodchuck said nothing. He was embarrassed to admit that he had not remembered.

"I had to talk to you," Weasel continued. "There is danger to you, maybe."

"Danger? I do not understand."

"You remember, back on the Great River, when you left the exploring party?"

"Yes, of course."

"There was danger, no?"

Woodchuck thought a moment, puzzled, but Pretty Weasel continued.

"You thought they would not understand, that you wanted to join your son."

Ah, *that* danger, thought Woodchuck. Technically, he was a deserter, and could be subject to disciplinary action. But, that was so long ago. True, the military had a tendency never to forget, but after more than ten years?

"But, Weasel, why now, why is there more danger now? Do they search for me?"

It still seemed unbelievable that the army would send an expedition half across the continent to capture one deserter. Or, maybe they knew that Lieutenant Du Pres was alive, and were after him, too.

"No, no, Woodchuck. They do not know you are here. This is just another exploring party. But the leader is Worm-Face."

Worm-Face! The energetic nobleman, bent on exploring the New World. Pierre, Marquis de Foixainne. The natives had observed his carefully trimmed and waxed moustache, and decided it looked like a pair of caterpillars on his upper lip. The soldiers had dreaded for the marquis to discover that he was called "Worm-Face," but when the time came, he was delighted. To be given a name was to achieve status, and the young marquis had been wise enough to understand it.

So, this was the danger. The marquis might recognize his former sergeant. Possibly even, since they had established trade with the Spanish, they could be charged with treason. Weasel was right. There could be much danger here.

"Is there anyone else who might know me?" he asked.

"I think not, Woodchuck. One or two of the voyageurs, maybe."

*Aiee*, thought Woodchuck. That is one or two too many. This could become very complicated.

# 7

>> >> >>

They talked a long time, sharing the stories of their lives since they parted on the Great River years before.

The marquis had insisted, related Pretty Weasel, that they comb the area for the missing sergeant. They had delayed an entire day, while everyone searched.

"Worm-Face was certain you had been killed by a bear or something," he chuckled. "I searched as hard as anyone. Finally we went on."

"And you found the Salt Water the Gulf?"

"Of course. Well, we did not go all the way. Close enough that natives along the river knew of it."

"Why not go on?"

"Woodchuck, you know Worm-Face is . . . well, different. Once he had proved it could be done, he was ready to try something else. Let others go to the Salt Water."

"So, you went back?"

"Not right then. We followed up several rivers for a few sleeps, then back to the Great River. Finally back to Mishi-ghan."

"You went with him? You did not go home?"

Weasel chuckled.

"It was exciting, following Worm-Face. I have seen much country, many places. I will go home someday, with tales to tell."

"But what are you doing here?"

33

"Oh. Worm-Face heard that the Spanish Hairfaces were here. He thought it would be good to trade with them, make friends with them against the English."

"Which way did you come?"

"By canoe, at first. Worm-Face thought we could go nearly here by water. We came up a river we called the Platte . . . very straight across flat land. Then we left the canoes, bought horses. We found the mountains, and traveled south to here."

"That was a long way, my friend," laughed Woodchuck. "There is a trail."

"From your country?"

"Yes! We learned of it, several years ago."

"You come to trade?"

"Yes. The People had no iron tools, knives, weapons. We have been trading each season, furs and robes."

Weasel nodded in understanding.

"Yes, I see. But, Woodchuck, it would be bad for Worm-Face to see you, no?"

Woodchuck was grateful that his friend had correctly understood that situation.

"That is true, Weasel. I must avoid him, and anyone else who knows me."

"Do you think you would be recognized?" Weasel asked. "You look much different."

"*You* recognized me," reminded Woodchuck.

"Yes," Weasel agreed, "but I do not know . . . you look like many other traders, now."

A shape materialized out of the darkness, and Pretty Weasel jumped in alarm. Woodchuck laughed softly.

"This is my friend, Sky-Eyes. He comes to take the next watch."

"Ah, yes," replied Weasel. "I have seen him. He looks more French than you."

The three discussed the situation. Only Woodchuck would be known to any of the French party. Therefore, he must avoid contact whenever possible. It would be wise, they decided, for Sky-Eyes also to avoid the French. His appearance was likely to raise questions.

Sky-Eyes was a trifle suspicious of the newcomer, however.

"Why should you help us?" he demanded.

Both the others chuckled.

"Because he is my friend," Woodchuck explained simply.

"Yes," added Pretty Weasel. "I tried to kill Woodchuck once, because I thought he was an enemy. He could have killed me, but did not."

"And then, Weasel helped me rejoin the People," Woodchuck finished.

The details were sketchy, but Sky-Eyes seemed partly convinced.

"But what are the French doing here?" he persisted.

"Worm-Face wanted to see if we could find them, the Spanish. Maybe set up some trade."

"Trade? From where?" Sky-Eyes asked in astonishment. "Are the French moving this far west?"

Weasel shrugged.

"Maybe, someday."

"I see."

So, there were plans for the future. Possible colonization. Sky-Eyes and Woodchuck looked at each other with some degree of concern. Once more, the question of divided loyalties had come up. Both men dreaded the changes that civilization would bring to the People. On the other hand, as trade expanded, the benefits of more easily accessible goods would be apparent. It was a dilemma that they could only hope would be a while in coming.

"Where are you camped?" Sky-Eyes asked.

"North of the town. We have been here only one day," Weasel responded.

Odd, thought Woodchuck. When we saw Diaz, he did not mention the presence of the French. Surely he would have done so if there had been formal contact.

"It is good," he told Weasel. "We thank you for the warning. I will try to stay away from any who might know me. Walk safely, my friend."

"You, also."

Pretty Weasel faded into the dimness of the night and was gone.

"Do you trust him?" Sky-Eyes asked.

"Of course. He could have just told the marquis without contacting me. Yes, I trust him!"

He was a trifle irritated that the loyalty of his friend would be questioned. Sky-Eyes noticed the irritation.

"Look, Woodchuck, I . . ."

"It is nothing. I know him, you do not."

Sky-Eyes realized that the less said the better, for the moment. He changed the subject.

"Well, get some sleep. In the morning, we trade. But, maybe you should stay in the camp, no?"

"Yes, I think so," Woodchuck agreed. "I will look after the horses."

He turned and made his way through the darkness to seek his sleeping robes.

# 8

>> >> >>

**G**round Squirrel watched as the trading progressed.
Gutierrez and Sky-Eyes, obviously good friends and vet-
erans of many sessions of trading, still haggled over each
pelt. It was, after all, much like the trading that took
place when they camped near the Head Splitters, their
allies. Both groups could hardly wait, it seemed, to begin
trading. Weapons, tools, skins, horses changed hands rapidly. It was a joke, not far from truth, that one man had
traded for three days, to end up with the same horse he
had owned when he started. ·

So, this was much the same. Ground Squirrel became
bored. He wandered around the store, examining the
wonders of unknown objects and utensils. He chose a
small ax for himself, and Sky-Eyes helped him trade for
it.

"Go ahead, you trade with him," Sky-Eyes urged.

"But I do not know Spanish."

"It is all right. Use sign talk."

"He knows sign talk?"

"Yes. Not many Spanish do, but Gutierrez does. It
helps him in trading. Tell him what you want."

Ground Squirrel, feeling more like a warrior with the
ax at his waist, strutted around the store a little while. He
was disappointed that no one seemed to notice, so he
wandered out the back door to watch the smith in the

yard. The man had strong medicine, able to heat, bend, and shape the hot metal.

Even that became boring after a while. He sauntered back through the store and looked out into the street. Maybe he could go for a walk. Sky-Eyes was busy. Turkey Foot dozed comfortably, squatting against the inside wall. It could do no harm, to look around a little.

He stepped into the street, squaring his shoulders and trying to think of himself as Red Feather instead of the baby-name Ground Squirrel. He even scowled a little, to look fierce and dangerous. He was quite aware of the shiny new ax at his waist, though no one else seemed to care. People in the street ignored him, or at best cast brief glances of curiosity at his unfamiliar garments.

He stared, in turn, at the closeness of the mud-brick lodges to each other. He still did not see how it was possible for people to live in such a dwelling, crowded together, with no chance for cooling breezes to refresh, no way to roll beneath the edge of a raised lodge-skin to get out in an emergency.

Ground Squirrel became aware of someone watching him. He turned, and saw a woman standing in the doorway of one of the lodges, leaning provocatively against the wooden frame. She beckoned to him, and he took a step or two in that direction. This would have to be a highly urgent situation, he told himself. Otherwise, the woman would not ask a stranger for help. At least, it would be so among the People. He saw that the woman was somewhat older than she appeared at first. She was not unattractive, however. She managed to show a considerable amount of skin on her upper chest and shoulders, shrugging suggestively at him. She smiled at him and extended her left foot, causing a shapely ankle to slide into view below her full skirt.

Ground Squirrel was aroused, but he was also confused. What was the nature of the woman's emergency? He stepped a bit closer. A sweet, provocative scent struck his nostrils, like the smell of flowers. As nice, almost, as the scent of the grape blossoms in spring, back in the Sacred Hills, the tallgrass country of home. Here, mixed with the musky smell of the woman herself, it was quite exciting.

She smiled and beckoned again. He saw that part of her beauty was achieved through the skillful use of face paint. Her lips and cheek bones had been reddened slightly, and he found the effect rather stimulating.

"Can I help you?" he blurted in his own tongue, realizing as he did so that she would probably not understand.

He tried again, in the Head Splitters' language and in sign talk. The woman only shook her head and answered in Spanish. *Aiee*, he *must* learn Spanish. The woman took his arm, and her hand was warm and exciting as she drew him into the doorway. She pointed to a bed against the far wall, and slowly began to unfasten the front of her skirt.

Ground Squirrel finally realized what was happening. *Aiee*, the woman wanted him in bed. He was aroused, and the prospect seemed exciting, but there was a doubt in his mind. He was unsure of the customs in Santa Fe. What if her man returned to find them so? Among the People, a husband might beat a wife found with another man, or mutilate her face to make her unattractive. True, it seldom happened. Not in his lifetime, anyway.

In some tribes, he knew, it was customary to share one's wife with a visitor, perhaps for a price. On the other hand, some, like the People, placed great emphasis on fidelity and the sanctity of marriage. Still others were quite vindictive toward the male transgressor, he had heard. Since he did not know the customs here . . . *aiee*, he had no desire to find himself suddenly seized and castrated like a young stallion of inferior quality. He turned and fled out the door, leaving the bewildered prostitute chuckling to herself at the never-ending variety of the male of the species.

Ground Squirrel had gone some distance before he paused to find his directions. He was a bit unsure of the way back to Gutierrez's store. If it had been in open country, there was no problem. He could find direction. Possibly it would take a little while, with the sun now directly overhead, but he could do it. But here . . . he began to panic again, feeling trapped among the threatening mud walls that prevented not only the movement of air, but the ability to see anything. He must get out, away and into open country. Then he could find their camp, and be back with his father, who had stayed with the horses. He did not quite understand why Woodchuck had stayed behind, but there must have been a reason. He had gathered that there was something odd going on, beyond the course of the usual trade. No one had said anything, to him, at least, but it was there . . . the feeling that both his father and Sky-Eyes were uneasy about something.

But, first things must come first. The few moments of wondering about his father's problems had eased his panic a little. Now he could rationally approach his own. Yes, his first move must be to escape the trapped feeling of the town.

He selected a street at random and jogged along between the mud lodges. Ah, yes, presently he saw open country ahead, and quickened his stride. The mud lodges became fewer, and he drew a breath of fresh air. It was not like that of home. The scents were different, there was an aromatic scent of cedars and juniper that was unusual at home, but it was the scent of the open, and it was good. He slowed to a walk and began to orient himself. Yes, there were the shapes of the hills to the north of town, which he had noticed as they approached. Now it was easier to establish directions. Yes, he had missed his way by perhaps a quarter of the circle, and was now to the northwest of town, rather than northeast. He had only to circle back to the east, around the town. Maybe he should get a little farther away from the outlying mud lodges, though.

He moved to the north, long strides covering distance, until another thought suddenly struck him. Sky-Eyes and the others would miss him, would be unaware that he had gone back to camp. They might take much time in searching. He should, of course, go back and tell them. He looked at the mud lodges below, and wondered if he could bring himself to go back.

These discouraged thoughts were interrupted by a reflection of sunlight from some bright object in front of him. He shifted his gaze and saw a metallic thing, partly covered in the sand, as if someone had stepped on it. Curious, he walked over to pick it up.

It was a medallion or talisman of some sort. Not a weapon, or tool, as far as he could judge. No, there were points on it, but none sharp enough to cut or scrape. It was much like a flower, as he turned it in his hands. Three petals pointing one direction, three smaller ones in another. Somewhat like the blue flowers which he had seen along the streams since they reached the mountains. The metal was silver-gray in color, not quite like that of the medicine knife. But, its medicine must be strong. He could practically feel it, lying in the palm of his hand. The surface was smooth and pleasant to feel as he stroked it gently. The owner of this medicine-thing must be greatly upset by its loss.

He looked around, and was surprised to see a man standing near, watching him. Ground Squirrel was confused, startled that someone had been able to approach him so quietly, unnoticed. The newcomer was of medium height, and wore greasy buckskins of an unfamiliar pattern. The man's hair, also, was trimmed and braided in a manner which he had never seen before.

Then, to his further astonishment, the man began sign talk.

"What do you have there?"

Pretty Weasel had been pleased, after his conversation
with Woodchuck. It had been possible to avoid contact
between his friend and his employer, who was also his
friend. It could have been trouble, this division of loyalties, and Weasel had learned to avoid trouble where he
could. It made life much easier.

As he had years before, Weasel understood Woodchuck's position. Loyalty to family and tribe was important. Of course, the French had been Woodchuck's tribe
once, but it was plain how his heart felt. He was now a
man of the Elk-dog People, and he, Pretty Weasel, must
respect that loyalty. At the same time, he must be loyal
to Worm-Face, the bold Frenchman for whom he had
great admiration.

To accomplish these purposes, the way of least conflict
seemed to be to avoid any meeting of the two parties. He
felt that he had now accomplished this. The trading
party from the plains would conduct their business and
be gone in a day or two, away from any chance contact
that might complicate the lives of them all.

The visit with Woodchuck had gone well, as he had
expected. Woodchuck, too, was one who would avoid
trouble where he could. Now, for the next day or two, all
that would be necessary was to keep the two parties on
different paths to avoid any chance meeting. So far, that
was going well. Today the traders from the plains would

be conducting their business with the trader, Gutierrez. What a strange name. These people all looked alike to him, and had strange names.

At any rate, the trading should be finished by evening, and the People would depart tomorrow morning. Meanwhile, Worm-Face was meeting at this very time with some chief of the Spanish. The marquis had excused Pretty Weasel from the meeting, though usually he participated in such conferences. This time there would be no point. Conversation would be carried on in Spanish, a tongue completely unknown to Weasel. Even sign talk was said to be used very little here in the southwest mountain country.

Weasel was pleased to be free of responsibility this morning. He had lost sleep, and was tired. He loafed around the camp, joked and gambled awhile with the voyageurs, and watched the sun climb slowly toward the top of the sky. It had been decided that all of the voyageurs would stay in camp until after the meeting of Worm-Face with the Spanish. Hopefully, they would be rewarded with a night on the town. Already there were ribald boasts and obscene jokes about the contemplated evening's entertainment.

Pretty Weasel had had freer rein to move about. Fortunately, as it happened. Otherwise he would not have chanced to see Woodchuck and the trading party in town.

Weasel became bored with the gambling, and dropped out of the game. He wandered around the camp a little, and watched one of the voyageurs cleaning his weapon. The muskets carried by these mercenaries had never ceased to amaze him. Their medicine was powerful, it could not be denied. With a crash like thunder, they could throw a small stone faster than the eye could follow. It was a very impressive ceremony.

Weasel had doubts about the practicality of these weapons and their medicine, however. The thunder-sticks were heavy, noisy, and smelly, and no more effective or accurate than an arrow, beyond a hundred paces. Even worse, they were slow. After the first shot, in the time required to ready the weapon again, a bowman would have loosed three or four arrows. Weasel had never seen these weapons used in combat. He hoped not to. Mostly they had been used to impress the local natives with a demonstration of powerful medicine when it seemed expedient.

One major disadvantage he had originally seen in the weapons was the necessity to stop and build a fire to ignite the match of each musket. To walk into battle with a burning rope in one's hand seemed ridiculous, anyway. On this latest expedition, however, the marquis had equipped his voyageurs with a new type. In this latest development, a metal disc whirled against a stone, showering sparks which ignited the medicine-powder. Worm-Face had offered Weasel one of the new thunder-sticks, but he had declined. He noticed that the voyageurs were not entirely pleased with the unpredictable function of the weapon, either. He wondered if the Spanish had this latest form of the thunder-stick. The soldiers he had seen in town appeared to carry the older type.

His mind wandered to other things, and he rose, a bit restless at the inactivity. Maybe he could walk toward town, see if anything was occurring that might be of interest.

And that was how he happened to encounter the young man who was just stooping to pick up something shiny from the ground. Weasel stood and watched for a moment as the other turned the object in his hands to examine it. Even at the distance of a few paces which separated them, Weasel identified the fleur-de-lis that was used as a mark or seal on the baggage and supplies of the marquis. Quickly, he realized that the seal must have been lost from one of the packs, and found by this youngster.

Next, Weasel turned his attention to the young man himself. The buckskins he wore seemed familiar in pattern. Ah, yes, like those worn by his friend Woodchuck. This, then, must be . . . yes, with a smile, he saw the family resemblance. This was the son Woodchuck had mentioned.

He wondered how much this young man (Red Feather was he called?), how much he knew of the intrigue involving the marquis. It could be much or little, he decided. No matter, it would be prudent to get him out of the area as quickly as possible. And how could they communicate? He had no idea whether the youth might speak French, the only possible tongue common to both. But wait! The sign talk. Yes, this young man had grown up on the plains. He should be adept at sign talk. Weasel waited until the other looked up and noticed the observer, then raised a right hand in greeting and began to sign.

"What do you have there?"

The youth looked startled for a moment, looked at the object in his hand, and then signed in reply.

"I do not know. I found it."

"How are you called?" Weasel asked.

"I am Red Feather, man of the Elk-dog People."

Ah, yes, Weasel thought. I was right.

"It is good," he signed. "I am Pretty Weasel. I know your father. But you should not be here. You must go. Here, I will take the thing."

He pointed to the fleur-de-lis seal. Red Feather looked at it again, shining in his palm.

"Is it yours?" he signed.

"Yes. My chief's. I will take it to him."

"No," Red Feather shook his head. "I will give it to him."

Pretty Weasel was becoming exasperated. He must convince the boy to leave quickly.

"No, no. You must not see him. You must not be here. Quickly, now, give it to me and go!"

Red Feather might easily have done so, but a slight stubborn streak in his makeup chose this moment to make its presence known.

"No! I do not know you, or whether you speak truth."

"I speak truth. I am your father's friend," Weasel pleaded.

The interchange was interrupted by the approach of one of the voyageurs.

"Ah, what have we here?" he spoke in French as he walked up.

Weasel stood, hesitating to answer, unsure how much to try to explain.

"*Mon dieu,*" exclaimed the voyageur, "he holds one of our seals! Where did you get that, boy?"

Weasel sighed deeply.

"He found it."

Then he turned again to the youth, using sign talk.

"See, this man knows the thing in your hand. It belongs to our chief."

"His chief and yours are the same? I think not," Red Feather signed scornfully.

"Yes, yes, they are French, like your father."

Instantly, Weasel knew he had made a mistake. Red Feather smiled broadly.

"Good. Then I will speak to the chief. He may know my father."

How ironic, Weasel thought. That, my boy, is exactly why you must *not* speak to him.

This exchange in sign talk was interrupted by the voyageur.

"Wait! Did he find it, or steal it? Has he been trying to steal our packs?"

He spoke heatedly, his animosity apparent.

Weasel shook his head helplessly.

"No, no, Luis, you have it wrong."

"Maybe we let the marquis decide, no?"

"No, let him return the seal to us, and go on his way."

Weasel motioned to the boy, and extended his hand for the seal. Red Feather, sensing the gravity of the situation, laid the object regretfully in the extended palm, and turned away.

"Wait," snapped the voyageur. "There is more to this than I can see. Do you know this boy?"

"No, of course not. I just saw him pick up the seal a moment ago."

"Still, there is something odd," mused the one called Luis. "It will be best to let the marquis decide. Tell the boy he is to come with us."

Weasel thought quickly, then turned to address Red Feather in sign talk.

"This one thinks you should meet our chief," he signed, indicating the voyageur. "You will come with us."

The three started back toward the camp of the marquis. Weasel noticed that the young man appeared wary, distrusting. How could it be otherwise, he asked himself. Even without understanding a word, Red Feather would have seen the enmity and suspicion expressed by the voyageur. Things had certainly become complicated in a hurry. And the marquis was not even in the camp. How could Red Feather be persuaded to wait, short of physical restraint?

They were entering the camp now, and the gamblers looked up expectantly, interested and puzzled about the identity of the newcomer.

"Check the packs," Luis called. "We may have a thief here."

This was going all wrong, thought Weasel. There was no need to approach the problem this way. Already uneasy, Red Feather looked around the group.

"You should give me your weapons," suggested Pretty Weasel in sign talk.

Red Feather bristled.

"I give up my weapons to no one," he signed.

Please, please, Weasel thought, give me the ax, don't upset these people.

"You must trust me," he pleaded. "I am your friend."

For a moment it appeared that Red Feather would agree. Then he became firm again.

"No," he signed emphatically.

He rested his hand on the ax at his belt. Some of the voyageurs apparently interpreted this as an aggressive action, and leaped to grab him. Red Feather wrestled free and turned to run, hands grabbing at him as he twisted away. Someone seized the ax, and knives flashed in the sunlight.

Red Feather sprinted out of camp, toward a broken,

rocky hillside. With horror, Weasel saw one of the voyageurs raise his musket.

"No, no!" Weasel yelled. "Don't shoot!"

The gun boomed, and the running youth seemed to stumble, slammed forward by the impact. Then Weasel's vision was obscured by the cloud of cottony smoke from the muzzle.

# 10

## 〉〉 〉〉 〉〉

**I**t had happened so rapidly that it was over before Red Feather could fully comprehend what had occurred. He heard the shouts behind him, and a boom like thunder. Simultaneously, something struck him in the back, a massive blow like that of a heavy war club. He stumbled and fell, but panic caused him to scramble forward, on all fours for a pace or two, then running again. There was very little pain, but a terrible shortness of breath. He could not draw in enough air to sustain his need.

The thought flickered through his mind that with the boom of the thunder, he had been struck by the real-fire from the sky. But something was not right. There were no clouds. Rain-maker was not at hand. No, he had been struck down by some powerful medicine in the possession of the men back there in the night camp. Men who, according to the stranger who had talked to him, were of his father's tribe.

No time to think of that now. He must run, get away from those who had tried to kill him. His right shoulder was beginning to throb now, and he glanced down, startled to see a spreading crimson stain just below his right nipple. *Aiee!* Had whatever struck him gone entirely through?

His thoughts were becoming fuzzy, and his legs seemed heavy as stone as he struggled to keep moving. There was a terrible hunger for air, a desperate futility that marked every ragged breath. Yet he must keep running. He could hear the distant shouts of the pursuers behind him. He must get away. They had tried to kill him once, and would do so again. He felt as a hunted animal must feel, frantically fleeing, aimless in direction, but running as long as he could move.

He saw broken rocks ahead, and turned toward that area. There he might find a hiding place, concealment in which to rest a little while. He scrambled into a crevice and rolled beneath an overhanging slab of stone.

His ears were filled with a roaring sound and his vision was blurred and indistinct. He closed his eyes. Was this how it felt to die? It took a few moments to realize that part of the sound was not inside his head, but in the crevice with him. The buzzing sound was familiar, somehow. He had heard it before. It was like the rustle of dry leaves, like . . . he opened his eyes, startled. Like the buzzing rattle of a real-snake.

The creature was scarcely an arm's length away, and he was looking squarely into the little old-man's face. He could see the black fork of the tongue flickering in and out between the lips as the snake stared at him, eye to eye. With great restraint, he lay as still as possible, taking care not to make any motion that would provoke the deadly strike.

He thought of his father. What would Woodchuck do? Woodchuck was well known in the tribe for his ability to talk to animals. Was there not a tale about a real-snake? He tried to remember. Yes, surely, there was such a story. What had his father said?

He began to talk, softly, slowly. He had little choice, because merely breathing had become a major effort.

"Little brother," he addressed the real-snake, "I am sorry to enter your lodge uninvited, but I must, in fear of my life."

The snake's hypnotic stare did not waver. Sweat formed in big droplets on Red Feather's brow.

"I will soon be gone, and leave your lodge," he wheezed, "but I must rest a little."

The buzz of the rattles slowed to a soft rustle and

stopped. Very slowly the tense attitude of the snake's neck began to soften. Sinuously, the coils loosened and the creature carefully slid toward a smaller crevice. It was not a retreat, merely a concession to circumstances. Red Feather watched the real-snake slide past his face, the body as thick as his arm. He was afraid his rough breathing would alarm the snake, and provoke it to strike, but he was unable to stop. He could not hold his breath. It was physically impossible not to strive for all the air he could gain. He felt like a fish, gasping helplessly on the bank while life slipped away.

After what seemed an interminable wait, the last tapering portion of the real-snake disappeared, with one last glimpse of the rattles as they slid from view. Red Feather relaxed somewhat, exhausted from his wound, his physical exertion, and the stress of the experience in the crevice. He had made his escape, but felt unsure, tired, and vulnerable. He wished for a passing moment that he could again merely be Ground Squirrel, the little Woodchuck, and be comforted in the arms of his mother.

Outside his hiding place he could hear his pursuers running, calling to each other, searching for him. He rolled slightly to one side and drew the knife from his waist. He would be ready to defend himself if he was discovered. He regretted the loss of the little ax, but there was not room to use it here, anyway.

The day dragged on, and the searchers sounded farther away now. He dozed fitfully, his back and shoulder cramped painfully in the narrow confines of the crevice. Consciousness ebbed and faded, blurring the passage of time, and he found it increasingly difficult to distinguish the ethereal dream-state from reality. Figures came and went, fluttering in and out of his mind.

He could still hear the voices of the searchers, dim and far away, when someone came and stood over him and peered into the crevice. With great effort he struggled toward the surface of consciousness, trying to focus on the face swimming before him. He readied his knife in a last futile defense.

*"Ah-koh!"* the figure whispered in greeting, at the same time signing for silence.

Red Feather saw that it was the man in buckskins, the one to whom he had handed the medicine-thing, the metal flower.

"Stay here," the man signed. "I will come back when it is safe. I will help you. Be very quiet."

There was a slight rustle as the man took a freshly cut branch of cedar and laid it over the opening of the crevice. Then he was gone.

Red Feather lay and pondered this for a time. He watched the light begin to fade through the feathery branch of the cedar, and wondered what the night would bring. He had no doubt that the man would return, probably before morning. The cedar branch would start to lose its freshness in the morning sun, and draw attention to the hiding place, so the man must intend to return before that.

But for what purpose? The stranger had talked of friendship, but had allowed him to be taken and injured with the thunder-medicine, whatever it was.

No, Red Feather decided, he could trust no one. Besides, he needed to vacate the lodge of the real-snake as he had promised. He did not know how long such hospitality might last. It was uncertain at best. One thing *was* certain. As soon as it was dark, he must leave his hiding place and hurry far away.

He slept for a little while, and opened his eyes. The patch of blue sky beyond the cedar branch was turning to pale blue-gray with the coming of night. He looked around the cleft. There was no sign of the real-snake, but the night creatures were coming awake. A small scorpion scuttled along the edge of the rock overhead and slipped out of sight. It would soon be time to move.

He listened carefully, and heard the hum of the night camp where the men who searched for him would be. A man laughed at some small joke. He tried to remember distance. The camp must be about a bow shot away, he thought. Far enough. The patch of sky was darker now, and he saw a star through the branch. It was time.

Carefully, he rolled out from under the ledge, pushing aside the branch with his good arm. He stood up, enjoying the cooling night breeze. He could see the sparkle of the distant camp fire, and the dim shapes of the rocks on the looming hillside. In the distance, a cluster of light marked the town's location.

He wondered where his own camp was located and what his people were doing. His father would be worried, he knew. They would have finished trading and found him gone. They would have looked for a little while, and then decided he had gone back to camp. When he was not there . . . well, there was no use in wondering.

He stood swaying, weak and dizzy. There was a warm trickle on his shirt, and he realized his wound had started to bleed again. Any effort, even that of standing, made breathing more difficult, but he *must* move. He stooped and replaced the cedar branch over the crevice.

"Thank you, my brother," he said softly to his unseen host.

Now, which way? He decided to try to circle the town, moving to the east, looking for the camp of his party. It took only a few paces, however, to become so short of breath that he knew he could never do it. Helplessly, he sat down on a sun-warmed rock, to catch his breath and devise another plan. If only he had a better idea of the direction he must follow. There was no room for error. He would have to be right the first time.

He stood again, unsteady on his feet, and moved forward. A dark shape moved in front of him, and he gasped in fright, hurting his sore chest. He doubled over, pain knifing through him and shutting off his precious air. The dark creature, as startled as he, gave a blowing snort of alarm, and shuffled aside. A horse! *Aiee,* this could make the difference, life or death. He moved toward the animal, talking softly, while the horse nervously moved away. It was hobbled, however, and he managed to throw an arm around its neck.

The effort caused him to stand gasping in pain. The animal, disturbed by the smell of blood, kept tossing its head, and the jerking motion seemed to tear his chest apart. Finally the creature quieted, and he began to evaluate the possibilities. There was the knife at his waist, and he drew it to cut the hobbles. But then, the horse would be free, and might bolt away. He could not risk it.

Carefully, he loosened the thong around his waist, and used it to form the medicine-loop around the lower jaw of the horse. He knotted it securely. Now he had control of the animal, and stooped to cut the hobbles free. There was a moment of blackness when he rose to full height again. He stood swaying, waiting for the faintness to pass.

He found it impossible to swing up onto the horse, so he led it to a large boulder, stepped up, and managed to half collapse across the animal's withers. His directions were confused, but he had enough presence of mind to turn the animal away from the French camp. Then he slipped into unconsciousness while the horse methodically plodded on.

It was not until much later that he discovered he had lost his knife.

# 11

>> >> >>

It was fortunate that the mare was well trained and cooperative. Even with the firm control of the thong around the lower jaw, Red Feather was in no condition to initiate such control. The animal moved along in the same direction it had started, at an easy swaying walk, the semiconscious rider slumping on its back.

Occasionally the horse stopped to browse on the scanty vegetation. Red Feather, roused by the change in the swaying motion, would speak or nudge the animal to move on. Slowly and erratically they moved eastward, through rocky country that was totally unfamiliar to Red Feather, even if he had been conscious.

It was about three nights past the full moon, and at moonrise the mare paused. They had arrived at a trail, and the animal had been given no direction which way to follow it. The rider, realizing only that they had come to a stop, mumbled to his mount, and without even raising his head, touched the horse's side.

They had approached the trail at an angle, and the portion that was more nearly straight ahead was to the left. The animal assumed that to be the rider's intention, and turned onto the trail, heading northeast. By the time the moon had fully risen, the trail was slipping smoothly behind. There was less opportunity for pausing to browse, and the mare continued to move along at a comfortable walk. The swaying motion was a lulling thing to

55

the senses of the desperately sick rider. He was no longer aware of anything that was occurring. The mountains were bathed in silvery moonlight, but he did not see.

Horse and rider moved steadily on, away from the sleeping town, away from the night camp where the voyageurs straggled back from town, laughing drunkenly as they sought their beds around the fire. They had discussed with wonder about the strange boy who had tried to steal their packs, had been shot down while escaping, and had then disappeared before their eyes. *Mon Dieu*, there was no end to the strange wonders of this land!

Pretty Weasel waited in his sleeping robes until the returning voyageurs began to quiet down. Finally, he rose with the rising of the moon and made his way out of the camp. Once clear, he changed direction and trotted to the crevice where he had found the wounded youth. Weasel was proud of that success. It had been difficult tracking, but he had seen the impact of the musket ball, and knew that there would be blood, if he could find it. That in itself was not easy. A droplet here, a tiny splash there, led him finally to the crevice. The boy looked weak, but sturdy, and he had further concealed the hiding place with the cedar branch, pretending to give up the search with the others.

Now he would assist the young man back to his father's camp. He removed the branch and bent to peer into the dim light of the crevice. He could not see well, and knelt while he moved aside to let the moon furnish better light. But the crevice was empty.

Weasel jumped to his feet, voicing an oath in his own tongue from half a continent away. Yes, this was the son of Woodchuck, as stubborn as his father. The boy must have gone to find the camp on his own. He had had the presence of mind to replace the cedar branch, so maybe the wound was not serious. In his heart, Weasel knew otherwise. He moved out at a trot, hurrying toward the other camp.

Some distance away, in the camp of the People, no one slept. There was much concern for Red Feather. They had finished the trading and found him nowhere around the store. Turkey Foot remembered that he had gone outside, so there was the possibility that he had returned to camp. However, his horse was still at Gutierrez's store. Alarmed now, Sky-Eyes sent Turkey Foot back to camp while he scouted the neighborhood in town. Both had no success.

They hurried to the Plaza to talk to Diaz, but the captain was out of his office. According to his clerk, he was attending some official meeting with the governor and some visiting dignitaries. Angry and frustrated, Sky-Eyes returned to search the town further, returning to camp only when darkness fell.

Woodchuck, of course, was distraught. It was all that Sky-Eyes could do to prevent him from rushing into town, or into the French camp, to demand the return of his son. Finally he was convinced, and they sat, sleepless, trying to decide how to start the search when daylight came.

There was a sound out in the night, away from the circle of the camp fire's light. Someone called out. They could make out a dim figure approaching in the moonlight.

"Ground Squirrel?" Woodchuck called out as he jumped to his feet. "Red Feather? Is it you?"

The newcomer strode straight into camp, and addressed Woodchuck.

"Is your son here?" Weasel spoke in French.

"No. Where is he?"

"I do not know. This is not good, my friend."

Quickly, Pretty Weasel related the events of the afternoon, and how he had helped conceal the boy.

"So, he was hit, but able to get away and hide. He was hit here." He pointed to his right breast.

"But why? Why did they shoot him?" Woodchuck pleaded tearfully.

Weasel shook his head helplessly.

"It was a misunderstanding. He was standing there with the fleur-de-lis . . ."

"It is no matter now," interrupted Sky-Eyes. "We must plan."

"Yes, I will go to them and explain," said Woodchuck.

"No!" Both Weasel and Sky-Eyes spoke at once.

"We can do nothing now," Weasel continued. "And you must stay away from the French. Let me begin, at daylight. I will track, starting at the cleft in the rock."

"It is good," agreed Sky-Eyes. "Except, we need a way to know what you are finding. Someone must go with you."

"I will go," said Woodchuck quickly.

"I think not, Woodchuck," advised Pretty Weasel. "You know . . ."

"He is right, Woodchuck," Sky-Eyes agreed. "I will go."

"No, that is the same problem," Weasel pointed out. "Maybe him," he suggested, indicating Turkey Foot.

"But he speaks no French."

"He does not need to speak French. He will talk only with me, and we will use sign talk."

The others began to see the advantage. Turkey Foot would appear to be simply what he was, a native trader from the plains. There would be no questions about his appearance or origin, and Weasel could communicate.

"It is good!" Turkey Foot nodded eagerly, pleased to be of help.

After discussion, it was decided that he would return with Weasel, and wait near the rock cleft for daylight. Then Weasel would join him and the two would begin to track the missing youth.

For the present, the others would remain in camp, but ready to move. Then Turkey Foot would return to bring them any news.

"Should we ask for the help of Diaz?" asked Woodchuck after the two scouts left.

"I think not," Sky-Eyes pondered. "That could lead to an incident between the French, the Spanish, and us. We do not want that. No, I think the quieter, the better. Let us see what they find."

Woodchuck noted that Sky-Eyes now seemed to trust the scout who worked for the French. That was good. The worst part, now, would be the waiting.

"Sky-Eyes," he said, after a long silence, "what do you think about this?"

"You mean, is he alive?"

"Yes. I have to think that. But, will they find him? Can he . . . oh, I do not know what I mean."

"My friend, I know this is a bad time," Sky-Eyes answered sympathetically. "We have seen other bad times together. But your son is clever, and strong, and Weasel saw him. He was doing well enough to escape. He may walk in here at any time."

Meanwhile, each step of the plodding mare carried the wounded Red Feather farther and farther away from those who sought to help him.

# 12

>> >> >>

The children of the People were excellent horsemen at a very young age. Many could ride skillfully almost before they could walk. This had come about as a result of a custom that was adopted generations before, shortly after the legendary Heads Off brought the First Horse.

It was found that infants enjoyed the gentle swaying motion of the horse's gait. It was much like the motion in a cradle-board, tied to mother's shoulders, and used for the very young. The cradle-board was impractical, however, for the mother of a young child while she was occupied with such tasks as skinning buffalo or dressing skins. Someone thought of a solution. A child could be tied on the back of a dependable old mare, which was then turned loose to graze. This early bonding between child and horse produced the finest horsemen the world has ever seen, the hard-riding fighter of the plains.

It was probably this culture trait among the People that kept the unconscious Red Feather on the back of his stolen horse through the night. Occasionally he would partially waken, mumble to the animal, and lapse back into oblivion. It was very little different here from the times his grandmother had tied him securely to a grazing mare to nap the afternoon away. The motion was reassuring, rocking him gently, stimulating him to keep breathing in and out. This alone may have kept him alive, helping injured lungs to draw in life-giving air, but preventing the gasping that had proved so self-defeating.

He was quite weak from loss of blood, and his body was crying out for rest. Surely, had he settled down to sleep without the rocking action, the lack of motion would have resulted in pneumonia by the time the sun rose. Even so, he became weaker and weaker.

Fortunately, the mare which had saved his life saw nothing strange in this situation. After the initial shock over the unfamiliar scent of human blood, there was nothing here that was unusual. There was a trail, wandering but well worn, one that could be easily followed without direction by the rider. Yet there was a rider, one who balanced limply, but adjusted to the trail.

Sometimes the mare paused to crop the scanty vegetation beside the trail. If she paused too long, the rider would rouse and speak or nudge her. So, nothing was different. This was a journey, at night, along a trail, nothing more, and she plodded on.

Once, she stopped, terrified at the distant scream of a great cat, the hunting cat of the mountains. Instinctively, she stood trembling at the unknown. The rider, who had not even heard the cougar's cry, roused at the sudden change in motion. He patted her neck in a clumsy, fumbling manner and mumbled to her incoherently. But, it was enough. Reassured, the mare moved on at a quickened pace.

The odd pair traversed areas of level ground, crossed the dry beds of small streams, and followed the trail along rough and rocky hillsides that sloped up and away to the mountains. The mare paused, just before daylight, and stood fetlock deep in the icy water of a stream while she drank deeply. This time the rider did not stir, and she moved on.

The sun rose, and a trio of noisy magpies startled the mare for a moment as they flew up almost from beneath her hooves. She sighed deeply. The animal probably wondered how long this unusual journey would last, if a horse wonders at such things.

Now the trail showed evidence of more use. It was

becoming uncomfortably warm as Sun Boy neared the top of his daily run. The mare paused more often to graze, but now the rider no longer stirred.

It was startling, then, when the rider suddenly dismounted. Not in the usual fashion, but sliding limply forward as the mare reached downhill for a mouthful of grass that grew almost out of reach. He landed with a thud, almost under the mare's front feet, and she jumped aside in alarm. She stood, snorting through flaring nostrils and staring at the crumpled form beside the trail, waiting to see what would happen next. But nothing did happen, and after a little while, the mare wandered off to look for better grazing.

"Look, father, a horse!" Moonflower pointed.

It was indeed a horse, Blue Corn saw, a well-built animal that he did not remember having seen before. The mare was grazing along the trail from Santa Fe, and he saw no one else. Most importantly, however, the animal was moving toward the bean field. She must be prevented from invading the crop. A single horse could easily lay waste such a field in a short while. He rose to go and investigate.

"Look! There is something in the horse's mouth!" Moonflower indicated as they approached.

"Yes. That is odd," her father pondered.

It was a thong, knotted around the lower jaw, as it was sometimes practiced by tribes from the plains. The medicine-knot, some called it, to allow control of the horse.

The mare was calm, and allowed herself to be caught without difficulty. This mare, Blue Corn realized, had been carrying a rider. No one would turn a horse loose with a medicine-knot in its mouth and the reins dragging. There was something wrong here.

He examined the horse again, and found a dark stain that spread on the sweaty shoulder, from the right side of the withers down to the upper foreleg. He touched it and his fingers came away reddened with a mixture of dried blood, now moistened with the damp sweat of the animal. The rider had been wounded, apparently, and had ridden for some time, or else had bled quite profusely. The mare herself seemed uninjured.

Blue Corn turned to look along the back trail. There was no indication of other riders. Had this one been alone? He saw no other evidence to supply any answers.

But wait . . . a circling buzzard, riding the wind currents high above, suddenly folded its wings and started downward in a long glide. Another altered the shape of its great circle to approach the area where its mate had descended.

Well, the rider was probably dead, but it would be well to go and see. It was not good to leave a dead person unburied, anyway. He started down the trail.

"May I go with you, Father?" Moonflower asked.

"No, I . . ." Well, why not? he thought. "Yes, come on."

The girl hurried after him. It was difficult to say no to this, his youngest child, and he loved to have her near him. So like her mother, the child had been. Now she was of marriageable age, and soon she would no longer be around to follow him and ask questions about the meaning of things.

There was no difficulty in finding the body of the fallen rider. A great black buzzard rose from a rock beside the trail, and flapped ponderously away when they approached. Another sat with head cocked to one side and eyed them suspiciously as they came nearer. Not until they actually neared the still figure did the bird rise into the air to beat its way upward.

"Be careful," Blue Corn warned as the girl ran forward. "We do not know . . ."

"Father!" she interrupted. "It is the son of your friend!"

Blue Corn hurried to kneel at the young man's side. There was no sign of life, and the color of the skin was ashen. An ominous stain darkened the right side of the buckskin shirt, black where it had already dried. He rolled the still form to lie on its back, and put his ear to the chest. No, it was too late. He started to give up the futile effort, but paused a moment. Was it . . . yes! As

faint as the flutter of a butterfly's wing, the distant sound
of a beating heart!

"He still lives!" he marveled. "But not much longer, I
am afraid."

He straightened and looked at his daughter. He had
not been unaware of the attraction between these two,
the evening that the travelers had spent with them.

"I am sorry," he said sympathetically.

Moonflower dropped to her knees and took the limp
hand in hers. She held it a few moments and then raised
her face to her father's.

"No," she said firmly. "He is alive. I will take care of
him. I will not let him go."

Blue Corn stared in astonishment. His daughter had
never talked so.

"Very well," he said slowly. "I will help you."

# 13

>> >> >>

It was nearly midday before Turkey Foot trotted into camp. Everyone gathered quickly.

"Have you found him?" Woodchuck asked eagerly.

"No, but we have found his trail."

"Where?"

"Near the camp of the others."

"But what . . ." Woodchuck began.

"Wait! Let him tell us! interrupted Sky-Eyes.

"Of course."

Woodchuck lapsed into frustrated silence.

"We met at daylight and started to look," Turkey Foot began. "We found the tracks of Ground Squirrel in the sand. It was not easy, because the others had walked . . ."

"Go on!" Woodchuck almost shouted.

"Oh. Yes . . . we followed a little distance. The tracks showed he was very weak. There was blood on a stone where he stopped to rest."

"He was bleeding?" Sky-Eyes asked.

"Not really. Not drops of blood. A smear, like his hand was bloody and he rested it on the stone. Partly dried, maybe."

"But he went on? Where?" Woodchuck demanded.

"Yes. He stole a horse."

"*Aiee!* That was a good plan!"

Turkey Foot nodded.

65

"We followed the trail of the horse," he continued. "It was moving well, so it seemed Ground Squirrel was able to ride."

"But where did he go?" Sky-Eyes asked, bewildered.

"That is the strange thing," Turkey Foot went on. "The horse moved east until it hit the trail, the one we came in on, and then they turned north."

"*North?*" Woodchuck asked in disbelief. "But why?"

"I do not know, Woodchuck. Maybe he goes home."

"Did you follow him to see?" Sky-Eyes inquired.

It was possible that the boy was confused, delirious, even. He might easily have done something of this sort that would seem completely irrational in the calm light of day.

"Yes, for a while," Turkey Foot was saying. "They kept heading on that trail, northeast. Weasel is following them. He sent me to bring you."

"Bring us?"

"Yes, Weasel thinks you should come. Oh, yes, the horse the boy stole belongs to the French."

"*Aiee!* How do you know?"

"Weasel says so. We found the hobbles where Ground Squirrel cut them off. Weasel knows the horse. A bay mare, paddles a little on the left front foot."

"Never mind the foot!" snapped Woodchuck. "Will they be after him?"

"Maybe so," Turkey Foot ventured. "But we changed the trail. Hid the hobbles, brushed over the tracks. It will be hard to find," he chuckled.

"But will they *try?*"

"Yes, maybe. But Woodchuck, they have no tracker. Weasel is gone, helping us."

"Whose horse is it?" asked Sky-Eyes.

That could make a lot of difference. If it was the prized mount of the leader, the situation was far different than if it belonged to an underling.

"I do not know," Turkey Foot admitted. "One of the warriors, maybe."

At least if it had belonged to the leader, Weasel would

have said so. There was no guarantee that the French would not follow, but it seemed less likely now.

The packs were already tied, and it remained only to load them on the horses. That work was quickly accomplished.

"Weasel wants us to bring an extra horse," Turkey Foot called. "He is on foot."

"There are two extra pack horses," observed Woodchuck, "but he may ride Ground Squirrel's horse until we find him."

Quickly, they mounted and started up the trail. Normally, they would have gone to say good-bye to Diaz and Gutierrez, but these were not normal times. Both men knew of their situation, and anyway, Weasel could carry news back. If, of course, there was any news to carry.

The animals, experienced in the routine of pack travel, moved out well. Even so, they did not overtake Pretty Weasel until well into the afternoon. He was moving rapidly, pausing only to verify his impression that the mare was following the trail.

"Ah, Woodchuck!" he greeted as they approached. "It is good that you are here. Look, I will show you."

He pointed out the tracks in the well-beaten dust of the trail.

"See, the left front? The mare swings that foot a little, so the track is blurred when she picks it up. But she moves well. A good mare. She will take care of a rider."

"But what of my son?" Woodchuck burst out.

"Ah, yes, I know your heart is heavy, my friend. And your worry is with reason. Look, the mare wanders, from side to side of the trail. She stops to take a bite."

He pointed to a tuft of freshly cropped grass in a cleft of the rock.

"Do we know," Woodchuck asked irritably, "that he is still on the horse at all?"

Weasel looked at his friend with sympathy.

"Yes, Woodchuck. I have followed this mare's tracks since he caught her before daylight. There was no place where he got off. Then, too, she keeps moving. Without a rider, she would act differently. She would stop to graze, or wander off the trail. No, she still carries him. But, he is not alert. He lets her wander a little.''

Tears came to Woodchuck's eyes, and Weasel reached to touch his arm.

"We will find him, my friend. Come, where is my horse? The day grows long.''

Pretty Weasel mounted and moved on, scanning the trail ahead of his horse, while the others followed a short distance behind. A time or two, he paused and motioned the others to keep back until he relocated the track. Once, at a rocky stretch, he stopped the party entirely and called Turkey Foot forward to help him search.

Late in the afternoon, with the shadow of the mountains sliding out onto the plain, he stopped and rode back.

"We should stop for the night,'' he said simply.

"What have you found?'' Woodchuck demanded.

"Come. I will show you.''

He dismounted and led the way on foot. Woodchuck could see nothing unusual at first. There were hoof prints that might have belonged to the mare.

"See,'' pointed Weasel, "the mare came over here and reached . . . no, stay back . . . reached for that clump of grass down the slope.''

Yes, Woodchuck could see it, now that it had been shown him.

"Then she jumped,'' Weasel continued, "over that way. What scared her?''

Without waiting for the answer, he continued.

"The rider fell off, here. See, the smooth place where someone lay? Now, somebody came from that way.'' He pointed down the trail. "Two people. A man and a smaller person, a woman or a boy. They stood here, made these footprints.''

"What then?''

"They took him that way. He was alive, because they took him on a pole-drag behind a horse.''

Weasel pointed to the pair of wavering grooves in the trail, where the ends of the drag-poles had trailed.

"How do you know that?'' Woodchuck asked.

Weasel shrugged.

"If he was dead, they would pack him on the horse. No, he was alive but sick, so they brought the pole-drag to carry him."

"Then, let us follow."

"No, Woodchuck. We do not know who they are, or where they were going. We might miss them in the dark. They are taking care of him. Let us camp here. We will go on in the morning, but we must not go into the unknown in the dark."

"But Weasel! We are almost to the village of Blue Corn, our friend. Let us go on. They will know who has taken my son."

"That is true, Weasel," spoke Sky-Eyes. "It is not far. It was probably someone from their village who found him."

"Oh. I did not know. You know these people?"

"Of course. We stay there when we travel."

"It is good. Let us go on."

# 14
## >> >> >>

**M**oonflower and her father had placed the unconscious youth on a blanket and lifted him gently to the
pole-drag. His breathing was still rough and shallow, his
pulse thready and weak.

"I am afraid it is no use, my child," Blue Corn cautioned.

"No, Father, we will help him," the girl insisted. "See,
he tries to speak."

Blue Corn nodded absently as he turned to lead the
horse toward the pueblo. He had heard the low moaning
sound that the injured man was making, every few
breaths. He feared that it was not an attempt to speak,
but rather the relaxation of the throat muscles as the
unconsciousness deepened. More like the death rattle
just before the spirit crosses over.

Patiently, he led the horse while Moonflower walked
beside the pallet. He was afraid that the girl had attempted more than she could accomplish, and his heart
was heavy. It would be sad for her when the boy died.
More especially, because the two young people had only
begun to notice each other. Blue Corn had been pleased
to meet the son of his friend, and proud that the two had
shown interest. He had some regret that the boy was an
outsider, from a far tribe, but that was a small thing.
There was no suitable young man in this village for his
daughter, who should be selecting a husband soon. The

outsiders who came trading each year had been friendly and honest, and brought gifts to show that their hearts were good. Yes, he had thought, this would not be an entirely undesirable thing.

They were nearing the house, and his wife came from the door, an anxious look on her face.

"What is it?" she called.

"He is hurt, Mother," Moonflower answered. "It is the one who was our guest!"

"Ah, no! Woodchuck's son?"

"Yes, Mother. I will take care of him."

Blue Corn's eyes met those of his wife, and he shook his head hopelessly. He shrugged to indicate that he had tried to dissuade the girl, but had failed.

"Very well," Pretty Blanket said crisply. "Bring him inside. We will try."

They carried him into the cool of the adobe structure and stretched him on blankets. Blue Corn attempted to remove the buckskin shirt, but finally cut it away. It could be resewn if need be, though there seemed little chance that the boy would have use for it again.

"What is his name?" Pretty Blanket asked. "I have forgotten."

"Red Feather," answered the girl.

"Yes," nodded her father. "He has been called Ground Squirrel, because that is a small woodchuck, and he looks like his father. Now that he is grown, he wishes to be called by his given name, Red Feather. The other is a childhood name."

Moonflower gently stroked the cheek of the unconscious Red Feather. Yes, she said to herself, asleep and helpless, he still looks like a child.

"Moonflower," her mother spoke, "go and bring the Elder."

For an instant, Blue Corn thought that the girl would refuse, to avoid leaving the injured youth. But her judgment quickly told her that they must have help. She jumped to her feet and ran out into the glare of the sun.

In a short while, she returned with the man of medicines. He carried a pack in his hand, which he set down beside the pallet. Quickly, he examined the limp form, lifting the patient gently to note the two wounds, front and back.

"What made the wounds?" he asked.

"We do not know," Blue Corn answered. "It was so, when we found him."

The medicine man nodded.

"Maybe the thunder-stick?"

"Maybe. He came from the direction of Santa Fe."

The man nodded again, and began to take things from his pack. He mixed dried plant materials, grinding them together in a bowl, adding a little water and small pinches of unknown substances. Then he prepared two poultices, for the front and the back of the chest, and with the help of Blue Corn, lifted Red Feather to apply them. He bound them tightly with a strip of cloth, and they gently eased the patient back to the blanket.

"He breathes more easily already!" Moonflower observed.

Blue Corn was afraid that it was only because the holes no longer sucked air, being plugged by the poultices, but he said nothing. The medicine man sang a ritual chant with rattles and a small drum, and then prepared to leave.

"I will return tonight," he said. "If he wakes, give him some soup."

Blue Corn followed him outside, and the medicine man turned.

"My friend, this boy is very sick."

"I know."

"Who is he?"

"The son of a friend. We wish to do all we can."

"Yes."

He paused a few moments.

"Blue Corn, you know that there are things of the body and those of the spirit, and they are much the same, but different."

Blue Corn nodded, silently.

"I have done the things I can for this boy, but . . . somehow, I cannot reach his spirit. Is he Spanish?"

"No. He is from a tribe of the plains."

"Good. There is a man at Taos, of our people, one who is very close to the things of the spirit. He is one of the youngest of the Elder Brothers, but he is wise beyond his years. He might be able to reach the spirit of this one, if he would come."

"Why do you ask if the boy is Spanish?"

"Oh." The medicine man smiled. "Popé . . . that is his name, this man at Taos . . . he hates the Spanish. He says they try to force their gods on us, and this makes us forget the things of the spirit."

"And you think he might help us?"

"I do not know. But this spirit is a stubborn one, and it is nearly ready to cross over. I cannot reach it."

"Then I will go to Taos."

"Good. Tell Popé I sent you. Tell him I will help with the ceremony if he will come."

Quickly, Blue Corn explained to the women, and brought the horse around to the door.

"I will be back as soon as I can."

He was not an experienced rider, but the horse was cooperative. It was plain that they should not push too hard through the heat of the day, but Blue Corn moved on, stopping occasionally to rest the tired mare and his own aching body. The trail was an ancient one, little known and little used. It had probably been known to the Old Ones, who had built the houses on the cliffs and then disappeared. Legend said they were the ancestors of Blue Corn's people, but others said they were another tribe entirely. It was no matter at the moment.

The trail led basically north, but wandered through the mountains and across forgotten passes to approach the pueblo of Taos. Blue Corn tried to judge when he might arrive there. Surely not before night had come. He paused to let the mare drink at a mountain stream, and took a long draught himself. It was difficult to remount, as his stiffening muscles protested the unaccustomed strain.

It was fully dark when he crossed the stream and approached the nearest houses.

"Popé?" he inquired of the man who came to the doorway.

"Over there," the man pointed.

Blue Corn slid to the ground and staggered toward the small structure, nestled against its companions.

"Popé?" he called.

A man looked out, and beckoned him inside. Blinking, even in the dim light of the fire, Blue Corn looked around. It was a quite ordinary room, with the usual strings of red chiles and onions hanging from the rafter poles. There were also assorted herbs, tied in bunches and drying for use in the ceremonies that were this man's profession. The strange yet somehow familiar smells of the place conjured pictures in his mind of open skies and far mountains.

"I have expected you," said the deep voice of his host.

Blue Corn turned. Popé looked even younger than he had expected. In the dark pools of his eyes, however, was an ageless wisdom. Blue Corn, though old enough to be the man's father, felt that he had entered the presence of someone in authority. It was seldom he had felt like this. The medicine man's gaze seemed to probe completely through him, to understand the innermost secrets of his very soul. Yet the gaze, so authoritative, was somehow gentle, comforting.

"I am Blue Corn. I was told you might help me."

"Yes? What is the problem?"

Quickly, Blue Corn related the circumstances of his journey to Taos.

"Can you help us?" he finished.

Popé nodded in understanding.

"Maybe. Much depends on this boy's spirit. We will see."

In a short while, he was ready to travel. A woman handed him a pack as he mounted his horse, and he tied it behind the saddle.

Blue Corn dreaded the rough journey back across the mountains, but there seemed no other alternative. Stiffly, he remounted the tired mare.

"We will be there soon after daylight," Popé commented. "I hope it is soon enough."

They rode awhile in silence and finally Blue Corn had to ask a question.

"You said you had been expecting me. How can that be?"

The young medicine man smiled in the dim starlight.

"Who knows? I was expecting someone. His spirit was reaching out to me for help. I did not know who it was, that it was you, or the trouble you would have. Just that you were coming."

# 15

### »» »» »»

Shadows were long when Sky-Eyes, Woodchuck, and the others approached the pueblo just before dark. Woodchuck kicked his horse into a lope, the last few hundred paces, and slid to a stop before the lodge of their friend Blue Corn. Pretty Blanket met him at the doorway.

*"Buenos días, señora,"* he greeted. "Do you know of my son?"

"Yes, Woodchuck. He is here. But he is not good. Come in."

Woodchuck was shocked at the appearance of the boy. He had never, except in the presence of death itself, seen anyone with color so poor. Moonflower, kneeling beside the pallet, looked up at him with tragedy in her eyes.

"He is dead?" Woodchuck mumbled.

"No, he still lives, but by only a little. Moonflower and my husband found him. He has been like this since."

Woodchuck noted the rude bandages, and the greenish paste extruding from the poultice on the chest. He looked inquiringly at the woman.

"The medicine man was here," Pretty Blanket explained. "He says that it is a thing of the spirit now."

Woodchuck looked around.

"Where is Blue Corn?" he inquired.

"He rode to bring help. There is a young man in Taos, one of the Elder Brothers, who is skilled in things of the spirit."

"He can help my son?"

"I do not know, Woodchuck. If anyone knows, it is this man."

"And Blue Corn will bring him back?"

Pretty Blanket nodded.

"He wishes to do so. They could not reach here before tomorrow."

Woodchuck went back outside to inform the others.

"We will camp by the stream," Sky-Eyes pointed. "My friend, our hearts are with you tonight."

He touched Woodchuck's arm sympathetically.

"Thank you, André. I will stay inside with my son."

"Of course."

"Woodchuck," Pretty Weasel spoke, in French, "could you ask what happened to the horse?"

Woodchuck turned and relayed the question in Spanish.

"Was the boy riding a horse when they found him, Mother?"

"Yes," she nodded. "He had fallen off. They found the horse first."

"What happened to the horse?"

"Blue Corn has it, to ride to Taos. He had no other. Is this not right?"

Concern showed in her face.

"Yes, yes, it is good," he reassured her. "Our friend Weasel only wondered what became of it."

To himself, he thought rapidly. If Weasel would ask about the horse at such a time, he must think it important. Was there something here that did not meet the eye?

As the party broke away to move toward the campsite, Woodchuck sought out Pretty Weasel.

"Why did you ask of the horse?"

"No reason, really," Weasel answered. "If I go back, I will return it."

Ah, there might be something else, it seemed.

"Weasel, whose horse is it?"

"One of the voyageurs."

"Then what . . ."

"My friend," Weasel explained, "look at it from their point. Here was a young man who may have been stealing . . ."

"But he was not!" snapped Woodchuck.

"True. You and I know that, but he was seen holding the fleur-de-lis, the seal from the marquis's baggage. Then he attempted to escape, and stole a horse. What would you do, if it was your horse?"

Woodchuck nodded.

"I would track down the thief."

"Yes. So would Luis, I think. So, as soon as I can, I will ride the mare back. Maybe I can say she wandered off, and I followed."

"I see. Thank you, my friend."

So, Weasel *was* concerned that they might be followed. This could be a grave danger. Aside from the possible risk of being accused as deserters, there was another danger. If the marquis' crew of rugged mercenaries decided on vengeance against the party of traders from the plains . . . *aiee!* Merely the fact that Ground Squirrel, suspected of thievery, guilty of horse stealing, was one of this party might incite an attack by the French. How ironic, that their greatest danger might prove to be from this unexpected source. In a country full of danger, peopled with unpredictable tribes and the unpredictable Spanish, their major threat was now from his own countrymen. And, outnumbered maybe three to one . . .

He wanted to talk to Sky-Eyes about it, but in the confusion of making camp in the darkening evening, opportunity did not arise. Woodchuck turned and went back to the lodge.

Through the long night, he sat or knelt by the side of Ground Squirrel, watching his son breathe in and out. Red Feather, he told himself, not Ground Squirrel. Yet, it was so easy to think of the boy by the childhood name, lying there so young and helpless.

Moonflower, too, sat by the patient's side, alert for any sign of change. From time to time she wiped his face and forehead with a damp cloth. Woodchuck studied the girl. He had noticed that the two young people found a way to communicate, the evening the travelers had stopped here.

She was beautiful, there in the firelight as she ministered to the unconscious young man. The look of wisdom and compassion on her face was beyond her years. Her beauty was not like that of the People, Woodchuck noted. The women of the People were noted, even among other tribes, for their beauty of face and form. Tall, willowy, and long-legged, in times past their girls had been stolen by their enemies to take as wives when opportunity offered. "Our women are prettier than theirs" was the time-honored explanation. Both Pale Star and Yellow Head, Woodchuck's own wife, were strikingly beautiful women, even by European standards. The striking facial features, the high cheekbones and wide-set eyes gave these women a special, regal appearance. The look of eagles, Looks Far, medicine man of the People, had once called it.

The pueblo people had an entirely different look about them, Woodchuck decided. He had never stopped to consider it before. They were long-waisted but shorter of limb, perhaps. The facial structure was broader through the cheeks, round rather than long. He studied Moonflower, unobserved, as she ministered to Ground . . . to Red Feather. Yes, her beauty would rank among the highest of all the women he had ever seen, but it was different. An open, friendly face, full of understanding and good humor, ready to smile or laugh when occasion offered. Just now, there was no occasion for joy.

The girl became aware that he was watching, and looked up with a self-conscious smile.

"He is no worse," she observed in sign talk.

Or no better, either, Woodchuck thought to himself. But, the girl was trying to help him. It might pass the long night of waiting if they could talk.

"You speak Spanish?" he asked.

"Only a little."

"But you know sign talk, no?"

"Yes, some."

Maybe he could use the unlikely combination of sign talk and Spanish to talk to her.

"I thank you for your help," he offered, using both.

She smiled sympathetically.

"It is nothing," she said in Spanish.

She paused, hesitated a moment, and spoke again, this time in sign talk, with which she seemed more comfortable.

"It is for him, but for myself, also."

She dropped her eyes, embarrassed.

"It is good," he said in Spanish.

Moonflower smiled at him again.

"Do you know what happened?"

"Yes. There was a mistake. Someone thought he was stealing."

"They hit him with the thunder-stick? The Spanish?"

"Not the Spanish. Another tribe. They have thunder-sticks too."

He had been searching for a way to indicate the French, but was at a loss. There was no way to sign for a people the girl had never heard of. Certainly, he could not tell her that the other tribe with thunder-sticks was the one from which he himself had come, his own people and those of Sky-Eyes.

"Was he stealing from that tribe?" the girl asked innocently.

"No. It was a mistake. He stole only the horse, to escape, after he was wounded."

Moonflower nodded.

"Tell me," Woodchuck pursued, "do you know this medicine man at Taos?"

"I have heard of him. His medicine is very powerful. He knows the ways of the spirits. He will help Red Feather."

There was something about the way the girl spoke and signed the simple statement that made the hairs prickle on the back of Woodchuck's neck. It was so straightforward, so matter-of-fact, as if communion with the spirits was commonplace. It was almost believable that it *was*.

# 16
>> >> >>

**W**oodchuck was asleep when Blue Corn returned from Taos, bringing the medicine man. He had thought that he would not sleep, and for a long time he did not. Pretty Blanket had lain down across the room, and seemed to sleep lightly, from time to time. Woodchuck had no desire to sleep. He talked with Moonflower, or watched her tenderly care for his son. A time or two the girl suggested that he close his eyes to rest, but he declined.

It was nearly morning when she spoke more forcefully. "Woodchuck, you cannot help Red Feather if you are sick yourself. He may need you. Here, rest a little. If there is a change, I will waken you."

She offered him a blanket and he lay down, certain that he would only close his eyes for a few moments.

When he woke, the sun was already up, and it was broad daylight. He could not believe he had slept. But, he realized, there had been no sleep the previous night, either. Sooner or later the body must admit its mortality and recover from such abuse.

Three men were just entering the door. One was Blue Corn, but the other two were strangers. However, it could be told at a glance which was the man from Taos. His very being radiated a sensation of spiritual excitement and power. Woodchuck had noticed this characteristic before. Looks Far possessed it. To a lesser extent, another or two in his past had also had this quality. In a room full of people, even a stranger would pick out this man as one of importance. His presence seemed to dominate the room, here in the lodge of Blue Corn.

When Popé turned to look at Woodchuck, the large dark eyes seemed to burn through him. Woodchuck felt that the man could read every guilty secret, every misdeed of his entire life.

"You are his father?" the deep voice asked in Spanish.

It was more a statement than a question, and it was plain he resented the necessity to use that detested tongue.

Woodchuck nodded, self-consciously.

"I am glad you have come, my friend," Blue Corn spoke wearily. "We have done our best for your son."

Blue Corn looked exhausted, bone-weary from lack of sleep, and travel-worn. He pointed to the others.

"This is our own medicine man, and Popé, from Taos."

"Yes, I have heard of Popé," Woodchuck acknowledged.

Popé looked around sharply, as if he doubted the statement, but then seemed to relax a trifle. He turned to the still form on the pallet. After a little while, he rose, and ignoring the others, spoke to the other medicine man at length in their own tongue.

For a moment, it appeared that Moonflower was about to speak, but then she sank back, dejected.

"What is it?" Woodchuck asked Blue Corn.

"They will take him to the *kiva*, the place of ceremony, a sacred place," he answered. "My daughter is unhappy, because she cannot be with him. Only men may enter there."

"May I go with him?"

There was a brief consultation, and then Blue Corn turned to Woodchuck again.

"Yes, since the ceremony is for your son. The presence of your spirit may help him."

It had become apparent that the two medicine men were not going to speak Spanish to Woodchuck again.

Maybe, he thought, it would interfere with their spiritual mood as they began the ceremony.

"What will they do?" he asked.

"I do not know, Woodchuck. Popé will try to call out to the spirit of your son, try to prevent it from crossing over."

"Can he do that?"

Blue Corn shrugged.

"Who knows? Maybe so, maybe not. Whatever is meant to be."

Moonflower was crying silently, large tears flowing down her cheeks, as preparations began to move the injured youth.

Woodchuck took her hand in his.

"I will be with him, little one."

One of the medicine men spoke crisply to the girl in their tongue, and she nodded.

"What did he say?" asked Woodchuck.

"That I must help. Try to let my spirit reach out after his."

Yes, thought Woodchuck. We must all pray for him.

Carefully, they lifted the unconscious form and carried him to the ceremonial area. This impressed Woodchuck as a sort of parade ground, with the sacred *kiva* near one end of the rectangle.

The sacred place itself was a circular pit, roofed over and with an entrance through which they now descended. It was steaming hot inside, as they ceremonially deposited the still figure near the center of the room. Popé turned to Woodchuck, and without a word, pointed to a place near the pallet. Woodchuck sat, while preparations quickly proceeded.

There was already an ethereal quality about the scene, a dreamlike feeling, complete with the sensation that everything was slowed until it seemed motion would stop. Later, Woodchuck realized that he could remember practically nothing of what had transpired. From the time when the preparations for the ceremony began, there was little memory. He would wonder later if this had occurred because of the great concern for his son's welfare.

However, he felt it quite possible that this was part of the ceremony, that he was not *intended* to remember.

He knew that there was a drum, tapped in cadence while Popé danced and chanted. A spectacular costume with a headdress or mask of some sort, rattles . . . beyond these fragmented bits and pieces, dimly remembered as from a dream, he could have told nothing.

He was aware that he had a strong impression for a time that there was a supernatural presence of some sort. It would be so easy, he remembered thinking, to slip over the edge and become part of it. But he did not know part of *what*, and he was a little bit afraid. There was a sense of anticipation. Not the possibility that some climactic event *might* happen, but the *expectation* that it would.

Then there came a rising climax to the chant and the drum cadence. There was a sudden shift in the tense emotion of the scene. His senses became more reliable again. He could feel the warm air of the *kiva*, and smell the unfamiliar smells. He was aware of the dim light, rays of sunlight filtering down into the room, marked by dancing particles of dust.

Popé sank to a sitting position, pale and exhausted. The ceremony had taken much from him.

Woodchuck was startled by a low moan. Red Feather moved in pain. It was hard to see his son in pain, but it was good. He knelt beside the pallet.

"You have come back to us," Woodchuck spoke softly.

Red Feather looked at him, with understanding in his eyes, but did not speak. The two medicine men were talking, in their own tongue, and Woodchuck could not understand, but he gathered that the ceremony had been successful. At any rate, his son was alive, and his eyes held recognition. For now, that was enough.

Red Feather drifted off to sleep, but now it was the healthy deep sleep of exhaustion. The breathing was deep and regular, not like the ragged gasps of last night. He stroked the sweating forehead, and found that the fever had broken.

"Sleep well, my son," he muttered.

He rose and faced the medicine man.

"Thank you," he said in the man's own tongue, one of the few phrases he knew.

He could not bring himself to address the medicine man in Spanish under these conditions.

Popé smiled and nodded, but did not answer aloud. Woodchuck looked over at Blue Corn.

"I will go and tell your daughter," he said.

"Wait. I will go with you."

Blue Corn rose.

Woodchuck was surprised to find that it was well past midday. They had been a long time in the *kiva*. The sun was warm, the air crystal-clear, and tasting good to the nose, mouth, and lungs. The two men walked in silence until they neared the dwelling, and Moonflower ran from the door.

"He is better!" she called. "I felt it happen!"

There was a wide smile on her face, tired but beautiful. *Aiee*, thought Woodchuck. Their spirits are that close?

# 17
>> >> >>

It was three days before Red Feather was able to sit up and take nourishment, but that did not matter to Woodchuck. His son was alive, and in his eyes was recognition and the will to live. The young man had been unable to speak at first, but this, too, returned, in no more than a day.

Moonflower seldom left his side, and Woodchuck watched the two carefully. It became apparent that the girl's strong will had been an important part of keeping Red Feather alive until the medicine man from Taos could be persuaded to come.

"She would not give up," Blue Corn told Woodchuck. "I was sure it was too late, but she would not let him go. She kept him alive, her spirit held him."

Woodchuck nodded.

"Theirs is a good meeting of the spirits, my friend. It is much like that of my own with his mother."

Blue Corn sighed deeply.

"Our tribes are very different. Will that trouble them, Woodchuck?"

Woodchuck smiled.

"I think nothing troubles them," he observed.

Then he became more serious.

"My friend, I can judge only by myself, but listen: I have had two wives, both of a tribe other than my own.

You know that I am a man of the People, but it was not always so."

"Yes. But that is an easy thing to forget."

"My first wife, the mother of Red Feather, I met before I was one of them, the People. That is how I joined my wife's tribe. She was more important to me than the whole world, but she was killed when our son was a baby. I tried to return to my own tribe, but came back, after several winters. On the way, I met my second wife; you know Yellow Head."

"Yes. A strong woman."

Woodchuck nodded.

"Yes, and now she, too, is more important to me . . ."

He paused, tears brimming up in his eyes.

"I needed her here with me when this trouble came."

This was a long and complicated conversation for the usually straightforward Woodchuck, and he felt that he was handling it poorly. He must make Blue Corn understand.

"So," he finished lamely, "they can know each other's spirit. Her tribe and his are not as different as mine was from the People."

Blue Corn nodded in understanding, but some doubt appeared to remain.

"Where would they live?"

Woodchuck had not considered this, and the thought was rather alarming. Among the People, it was common for a young husband to join the band of his wife's family, though there were exceptions. He felt unsure of the custom of this pueblo tribe. He had never wondered, until now.

"Maybe," he ventured, "they will let us know how it will be."

The two men smiled together, both a little uneasy about this unexpected development, but realizing there was probably little that they could do to interfere.

Popé, after assuring himself that the wounded youth was conscious and rational, quickly made preparations to leave. He brushed aside all offers of gifts from Woodchuck, except for some of symbolic usefulness.

"You will help me, later," he promised.

Once again, Woodchuck had the eerie feeling that this man saw things unseen by ordinary mortals. Possibly even things in the future?

Woodchuck did, during the days of inactivity, begin to carve a medicine stick, to be given to the man who had saved his son. It would be in his favorite design, an eagle. He had found this an impressive gift in any number of situations, and he felt that Popé would understand its significance.

Pretty Weasel, too, departed as soon as Red Feather seemed out of danger. He would return to the French party, riding the bay mare, with a story about having tracked the mare. He would say nothing about Red Feather.

"Will they believe you?" Sky-Eyes asked.

"Why not?" Weasel shrugged. "They maybe will not even ask. They are camped there so Worm-Face can hold council with the Spanish. That is more important than Weasel and a bay mare."

"How long will they stay?"

Weasel spread his palms helplessly.

"Who knows? Woodchuck, you know how Worm-Face is. If he is having a good time, he stays maybe half a moon, maybe all summer."

Still, the unpredictability of the situation was frustrating. It seemed likely that the marquis would break camp soon, and Weasel had little idea what his plans might be then. To add to this unknown factor was the incident involving Red Feather, and the further matter of the stolen horse. There was no guarantee that Weasel could convince the voyageurs that the horse had not been stolen, but had only wandered away.

Woodchuck talked with Sky-Eyes about the dilemma.

"Maybe it would be better for you to go on home," he suggested. "Red Feather and I could stay here, and follow when he is better."

"I think not, Woodchuck. It is better to stay together. He grows stronger, and we can travel soon."

It was agreed that, for the present, the trading party

would camp nearby, and wait to see Red Feather's progress.

"Maybe we will do some hunting in the mountains," Sky-Eyes suggested. "Do not be concerned about it, Woodchuck."

The days passed, and Red Feather grew slowly stronger. The others rested, gambled a little, and exchanged stories with the pueblo people. Occasionally they hunted, sharing their elk or venison with people of the village. It was a good time, with long summer days and cool nights, new friends to enjoy and no urgency to do anything else. Aside from the always-present desire to rejoin their families, the only marring thoughts that recurred from time to time were of the French. What were they doing? Had they left Santa Fe? When they did, which way would they go?

As each day passed, it seemed less likely that the French were interested in pursuit. If the owner of the horse had actually disbelieved the story told by Pretty Weasel, he would probably have followed at once. So, the incident must be forgotten. Each day became more reassuring.

Red Feather became stronger, walking around the lodge of Blue Corn at first. Then, day by day, he began to stroll slowly around the pueblo, along the stream, and to the camp of the trading party. In all of these exploratory forays, Moonflower was constantly at his side, guiding, supporting, encouraging. In the minds of everyone, the two became as one, inseparable.

Woodchuck watched them as they moved slowly along the stream one day, giggling and laughing like happy children. It had become a certainty now, the knowledge that these two would spend their lives together, though nothing had been said. Woodchuck wondered if he and Yellow Head were ready to give up their son. How much better, though, to give him up this way, to the happiness of his own lodge. For a time it had appeared . . . he shook his head to escape the unpleasant memories of the terrible days of uncertainty.

Nothing had been said by the young people as to their

plans. Would Red Feather stay here, or would Moon-flower go with them? Woodchuck knew that soon he must ask. They should be moving on, regardless.

He talked of the trail with Blue Corn. The pueblo people, too, knew it as an ancient trail, leading to the plains. Somewhat to his surprise, their host described an alternate branch.

"I have not used either trail," Blue Corn admitted. "My people do not travel much, like yours."

"But where is this trail?" Woodchuck asked.

"They separate a day, maybe two sleeps, from here. The Mountain Trail, the one you use, goes north over Raton Pass."

"And the other?"

"Yes, the Desert Trail. It leaves the main trail to go northeast. I have seen the place."

"But where does it go?"

"Across the desert. It is dangerous. There are rivers, but they run upside down, it is said."

Woodchuck recalled that he had heard this strange description before. In the northern reaches of the Head Splitters' range there were such streams. In the dry season, water must be obtained by digging in the dry sand of the river bed.

"That trail joins the other one again at a river on the plains," Blue Corn was saying. "I do not know its name."

"The *Ar-kenzes*," said Woodchuck, half to himself.

Yes, the Southwest Trail, from the Sacred Hills of the People to the town of Santa Fe, followed the *Ar-kenzes* for much of its length. It might be well to explore the possibility of a shortcut. In some seasons, it might be a valuable alternative route. And faster, if Blue Corn's information was accurate. He must talk with Sky-Eyes about this.

All of this discussion completely left his memory, however, when he rose next morning to see Red Feather sitting astride one of the horses. Moonflower held the bridle to help control the animal, but it seemed unnecessary. Red Feather sat confidently, smiling broadly.

"Father!" he called. "It is time we started home! I am hungry for hump ribs!"

The tears came to Woodchuck's eyes. One of his major questions was answered. Red Feather would be coming home with them, with his new bride.

"It is good!" he called enthusiastically.

Besides, what could be better to complete the youth's recovery than the curative powers of well-browned buffalo hump ribs? His mouth watered at the thought.

They were going home.

# 18
>> >> >>

**M**oonflower and Red Feather were united in marriage in the cool of the evening, beside the stream that flowed past the village. The murmur of the water was answered by the murmur of the breeze in the age-old cottonwoods that formed a canopy overhead.

Their traditional ceremonies were vastly different, those of the pueblo tribe and those of the Elk-dog People. So different, in fact, that it seemed prudent to use both, or at least a combination.

The couple knelt, side by side, while the fathers of both placed a blanket around their shoulders to symbolize the union. This approximated the ceremony of the People, with the bride's father drawing a buffalo robe around them.

There followed a modification of the ceremony of Moonflower's people, with the eating of symbolic corn cakes, and the sipping of water poured from a double-throated wedding pitcher. Appropriate remarks and ritual prayers by both fathers completed the ceremony. It was worthy of note that neither of the young people understood the words of the other parent. Their tongue of communication was not a tongue at all, but sign talk. Only a few words of Spanish were understood by both.

This did not seem, to the wedding couple, to present much of a problem. They had been together constantly, these past few days, and their communion was one of the spirit. They had watched the circling hawk high above, as well as the silvery minnows in the stream, and the fluffy white clouds over the distant mountains. They had laughed together with the joy of living, and knew that, although they could not tell each other in words, they had the same feelings.

Preparations were made for the party to move out at daybreak, to start the long trek home. Woodchuck was concerned, of course, that travel would be too much for his son, but it appeared that the recovery was going well. No bone had been injured, it seemed, and the recuperative powers of the young had helped to heal torn flesh and skin. Red Feather could now fill his lungs deeply, flinching only a little at the unaccustomed stretch of healing muscles. He had continued to spend increasing amounts of time on horseback during the few days prior to departure, with no ill effects.

Moonflower, unaccustomed to riding, was somewhat apprehensive about the project, but eager to try. Woodchuck and Sky-Eyes selected one of the pack horses, a comfortable, easygoing old gelding. They created a saddle pad, stuffed with dried grasses to provide comfort for the inexperienced girl.

Naturally athletic, Moonflower took naturally to the instruction of the men from the prairie, and soon proclaimed herself ready to travel. It was planned, however, to travel in easy stages, both for the girl and for the recovering Red Feather. There was no urgency in this journey, beyond that of the coming winter. If need be, they could stop for a time with the Head Splitters, the tribe of Turkey Foot and Lean Bear. It would also be possible to stop with the Red Rocks band of the People, to winter with them, even. Yes, things were moving nicely.

*Aiee,* thought Woodchuck. What a surprise, when Red Feather returns with a wife. This trip was to be an initiation into manhood for him, but . . . he smiled to himself at all the ribald jokes that would be directed toward the young man.

He noticed, also, that he was beginning to think of his son as Red Feather, not Ground Squirrel. A man who, after a moon's travel, has survived a wound from musket fire, recovered, and taken a wife should not bear a childish nickname.

Before departure, Woodchuck left two medicine sticks with Blue Corn. They were quite similar, both carved with an eagle's head and decorated with paints and strips of otter's fur. To these medicine sticks, Woodchuck added a touch he had not used before. He had noticed that in the mountain streams, there were often nests of tiny stones, worn perfectly round and polished by the centuries of motion. He had picked out and saved a handful of well-polished examples in different colors and shades, carefully matching them by pairs. These stones, chosen for appropriate size and a golden color, were used for the eyes of the carved eagle heads. A drop of pitch extruding from the trunk of a pine tree was used to cement each eye into a recessed wooden socket. Woodchuck was pleased with the effect, and with the admiration it produced in other people. Blue Corn was deeply touched, and it was plain that he would treasure the medicine stick forever. The second stick, he promised to send, or take, to Popé at the earliest opportunity.

"We will take the main trail, over the pass," Woodchuck told Blue Corn. "We know that way. But, sometime we may try the other."

It might be too risky to try the dangerous shortcut with Red Feather still recovering. Also, Moonflower was scarcely skilled enough with the horse to be attempting the trip at all. Blue Corn nodded in understanding. He was still concerned over the loss of his daughter.

"You will come back to visit?" Pretty Blanket asked her daughter.

"Of course, Mother. Next season. I will stay with you while they go on to trade."

It was barely full daylight when the party moved out. They would travel slowly, with frequent stops to rest. Even so, they made good time, and everyone was pleased that there were no problems.

When Woodchuck rose to relieve Lean Bear at the watch, he was ready to enjoy the night. The mountain breeze was cool and sweet-scented with a hint of pine. The stars were bright, and a slim crescent moon was sliding toward the western horizon. Woodchuck had never objected to night watch, even as a soldier in His Majesty's army. It was a time for thinking and meditation. He was looking forward to this night.

He spoke quietly as he approached the seated Lean Bear. It would not do to startle a man on watch. It was not unknown for a nervous soldier to panic and shoot his relief as he came on duty.

"Bear?" he called quietly.

"Yes. Over here."

Lean Bear did not rise, or even move, as Woodchuck came up to him and stopped. Woodchuck sensed that the man was uneasy.

"Is anything wrong?" he asked quietly.

"I do not know, Woodchuck," Bear said slowly. "Look, where the notch in the ridge meets the sky. About two hands left of that, and down a little."

Woodchuck extended his hand to arm's length, and measured. Yes, there was a pinpoint of light. It could have been a star, except that it was below the horizon.

"A camp fire?"

"Yes, maybe so."

"Could that be Blue Corn's village?"

"Maybe. It is nearly a day's journey away. But is not the village on the south slope of a hill? We should not see it from here."

"But that fire is on the trail, where we were today, no?" Woodchuck theorized.

"Yes, I think so," Lean Bear agreed.

"Then it is some other traveler, behind us on the trail."

"Yes."

This would not seem to be a discovery of earth-shaking importance, under usual conditions. The trail was often used, by many tribes and over eons of time. That was what made the trail. Moreover, the other travelers were a day behind them.

However, Woodchuck reminded himself, these were not usual conditions. They were traveling slowly, their travel crippled somewhat by Red Feather's partial disability and the girl's inexperience. They were not in a position to pursue either of the customary options, to run or to fight. Worst of all, the nagging thought kept returning to haunt him. The French, his own people (though that was unknown to them), had tried once to kill his son, and nearly succeeded. If they had discovered that he actually *had* stolen the bay mare, they still could be in pursuit.

He turned to look toward their camp. No, the fire could not be seen. It was behind the shoulder of the hill. At any rate, whoever spent the night at that camp on the back trail could not see the camp of the traders. But could it be the French? No, of course not, he told himself irritably. Just some traveler.

"Could it be the ones who shot your son?" asked Lean Bear innocently.

Woodchuck was startled. At least one other had considered the same possibility.

"Bear," he said seriously, "maybe we should talk to Sky-Eyes."

Lean Bear rose to his feet.

"I will bring him."

In a short while, the three stood watching the point of light.

"It is dying down, now," Lean Bear observed. "They are ready for sleep."

"What do you think, Sky-Eyes?" asked Woodchuck.

His friend gave a deep sigh.

"I think," he said slowly, "that we cannot afford to take chances. We must *know* who they are."

"How can we do that? We cannot wait here."

"Listen," Lean Bear spoke. "Let me go back to see. If I start now, I can catch up to you tomorrow night."

They discussed briefly. It might take longer than that, all agreed. It might be necessary to observe the other party at their next night camp. But the basic plan was good. They would rise at dawn and continue on the trail, not hurrying, but moving along. Meanwhile, Lean Bear would be scouting the mysterious followers on the back trail.

# 19

>> >> >>

**N**ext morning Sky-Eyes mentioned to the others that Lean Bear had gone scouting. This was not an unusual thing. Frequently a member of the party would be absent for half a day, riding ahead or to one side, a lookout for anything unusual.

It was a habit developed from centuries of nomadic travel on the plains. When a band of the People was on the move, scouts would be riding on the flanks and in front, to warn of any potential danger, or of game if it was appropriate. Unexpected confrontation, for instance, with one of the gigantic herds of migrating buffalo could be either a fortunate source of food for the winter, or a potential danger.

The outriders were called "wolves" by most of the tribes. Originally, somebody probably said it as a joke. There was a certain similarity between the scouts, circling the traveling column, and the ever-present gray wolves which attached themselves to a buffalo herd. Any sizable herd on the move was flanked by a few of the gray ghosts, circling and waiting for the weak, sick, or injured to fall aside. It made no difference that the purpose of the scouts was the opposite of the circling predators. The name stuck, and the joke became a part of the culture, its origins forgotten.

So, the party easily accepted the absence of Lean Bear. It was assumed he was acting as wolf today, and would rejoin them at the midday halt, or by evening. Woodchuck and Sky-Eyes had decided not to concern the others with the reason for Lean Bear's prolonged scout. It might be nothing, merely a party of travelers from one of the tribes of the area. In that case, there was no reason to let the others worry. If it seemed that there was an actual threat of danger, there would be time to explain.

They had, however, explained to Lean Bear the extra threat which the French might present, that of Woodchuck's status as a deserter. This was a difficult thing for Lean Bear to accept.

"They would have stopped you from leaving?"

"Yes, if they had known."

"Why?"

This was a difficult explanation, one which they were unprepared to discuss on the mountain in the middle of the night.

"It is their way!" Woodchuck stated in frustration.

Lean Bear stared at him, sympathy showing in his face even in the dim starlight.

"*Aiee,*" he said softly, "their ways are strange. I can understand why you left that tribe for your wife's people."

He shook his head again in disbelief.

"To not let a man do as he wishes!" he muttered, half to himself.

"It is no matter. Go, now!" Woodchuck insisted.

Still unconvinced, Lean Bear prepared to mount.

"It is like the Spanish, whose warriors must do as their subchief says?"

"Yes, something like that. Be careful, my friend."

"Of course."

He rode away on the back trail, still muttering about the strange ways of this unknown tribe. Sky-Eyes had returned to his sleeping robes, and Woodchuck resumed the watch.

The trail next morning was open and plain, marked by generations of moccasined feet. Travel was easy, as the sharp ascent into the mountains to cross the pass was still ahead. Woodchuck was pleased that Red Feather seemed to tolerate the travel even better than the day before. He was uneasy, however, about the back trail. He took the rear of the column, and frequently stopped to study the country behind them. He saw nothing. He did not actually expect to see anything, but he had to look, anyway. It was easy to see, in his mind's eye, the worst of circumstances. An accidental confrontation, Lean Bear unable to explain his presence, the vengeful mercenaries in the employ of the marquis . . . he should have gone himself, Woodchuck thought.

But no, that was ridiculous, he told himself. Lean Bear was noted for his scouting and tracking skills. He would not be caught unawares, even by the trail-wise voyageurs. This logic did little to reassure him, and he remained concerned through the day's travel.

They camped that evening near a small stream at the edge of a high, level plain, surrounded on the north, west, and south by foothills with sparse timber. They had traversed some hilly country through the afternoon, and it appeared that there would be more tomorrow. To the north, higher slopes beyond the first range led upward to where the trail would cross the pass. Then it would feel more like home.

To the northeast lay open plains, sloping away in the distance, already in the shadow of the peaks to the west, as the sun painted the sky orange and pink above blue mountains.

Lean Bear had not returned. No one mentioned his absence, assuming, apparently, that he would join them at night camp when he was ready. He should have no trouble finding the camp.

Turkey Foot had chosen the campsite, and Woodchuck was pleased that the fire would not be visible from the back trail. He might have argued over the selection, he thought, and was glad that it was unnecessary.

Woodchuck took the first watch, hoping to see some sign of Lean Bear before dark. In this he was disappointed. He sat watching the back trail, as the shadows darkened, changing from gray-blue to purple, and finally to black. Stars, only a few at first, began to multiply across the sky until they covered the entire expanse of velvety dark. Still there was no sign of Lean Bear.

He searched the distant landscape, in vain, for a sign of that pinpoint of light that would indicate the location of a camp fire. There was nothing. He told himself that it was of no importance, that there was probably no one on their back trail anyway, that the fire of the previous night was merely that of local inhabitants. How, then, the disconcerting thought came back at him, how is it that Lean Bear has not returned?

He worried and fretted until Turkey Foot came to relieve him.

"Anything?" Turkey Foot asked simply.

"No. Lean Bear has not come back. Did he come in the other way?"

Woodchuck was fairly certain that he had not, but must ask.

"Not while I was awake," yawned Turkey Foot, not troubled by his cousin's absence.

So, I should not be, either, Woodchuck tried to convince himself. He turned and moved toward the dying fire and his sleeping robe. But Turkey Foot does not know the nature of Bear's mission, he thought. Maybe I should go and look for him.

He was still standing, considering that idea, when Sky-Eyes materialized out of the darkness.

"How does it go?" he asked.

Woodchuck shrugged.

"Bear is not back."

"Can you see their night fire?"

"No. Nothing."

"Well, Bear is careful. He had much country to cover. It takes time."

"I thought I might go to look for him."

"And then we would have two to worry about? Two less in case of trouble here?"

"Of course. It would be foolish."

"Come, let us get some sleep."

The two returned to their robes, but it was long before Woodchuck slept. It seemed that he had just closed his eyes when someone shook him awake. Woodchuck reached for his knife in unconscious reflex, but a quiet voice spoke in reassurance.

"No, no, it is Lean Bear!"

Woodchuck relaxed and sat up. The sky was turning yellow-gray in the east, and the night was nearly over.

"*Aiee!* Bear, I was worried for you."

"Why? I was all right."

"What did you find?"

"I watched them as they traveled. They are the ones we talked of, your onetime tribe, who shot Red Feather. Your friend, Weasel, is with them. There are fifteen."

"Yes? Go on."

Lean Bear shrugged.

"I do not know, Woodchuck. They are strong, well armed, and well mounted. They travel fast. Faster than we can, I think. I had to wait till dark to get around them."

So, thought Woodchuck. We *are* pursued. Whether for himself and Sky-Eyes as deserters, or for the arrest of Red Feather as a thief, he did not know. It mattered little, now. They could not outrun their pursuers. To stand and fight would be out of the question, outnumbered three to one. He did not know whether he could bring himself to fight Frenchmen, anyway.

"How far are they?" he asked wearily.

"Half a day, maybe."

So little time. Maybe they could leave the trail, escape into the hills.

"We must talk to the others," Woodchuck said.

The camp was coming to life, men going out a little way to urinate and returning to prepare for the day's travel. There were joking calls to Lean Bear.

"Ah, Bear! What makes you so slow?"

"Come, everyone," Woodchuck motioned, "we must have council."

The joking stopped, and the party gathered in the growing light of dawn. Woodchuck explained the situation.

"We can fight them!" Turkey Foot exclaimed.

"No, there are too many, and they have thunder-sticks," reminded Sky-Eyes.

That was a sobering thought. There was silence for a moment.

"Should we split up? Go different ways?" Lean Bear suggested.

"No, we should stay together," Sky-Eyes stated. "But maybe we could hide while they pass."

That seemed unlikely, thought Woodchuck. He was standing on the west side of the circle, facing east, watching the yellow glow of the dawn spread along the horizon. He wondered, at what point would the flame of the rising sun first show itself?

The light just before dawn was always so deceptive, bathing everything in a golden glow, distorting distance and shape. The trail wandered to the north, toward the pass, and he wished that they were already over that ridge in the distance. Of course, it would do no good. Their pursuers would still be behind them, and gaining.

In frustration, he looked to the northeast to where he knew the Sacred Hills lay, far away, far across the prairie. For a moment, he thought his eyes were playing tricks. He saw a thing that he had overlooked the evening before, in the failing light of dusk.

"The Desert Trail!" he said softly.

# 20

>> >> >>

The Desert Trail was not plain to see. It appeared as a minor trail, one which seemed no different from some of the other local branches of the main trail. Woodchuck was certain, however, that this was the place, the fork of the trail described by Blue Corn. The lesser trail led away to the right, heading northeast, while the main path, the Mountain Trail, pointed nearly straight north. The eye could not follow the desert branch beyond a few hundred paces. It was soon lost in the gentle undulations of the land.

"What is it?" asked the puzzled Sky-Eyes. "What are you talking about?"

Woodchuck was excited now.

"Look, the trail that leads away from the mountains. Blue Corn told me of it. It is part of the trail to the plains, our Southwest Trail."

"But it leads nowhere."

"Yes, yes, it *does*. It is a shortcut. It meets the main trail, on the river in our country."

"The *Ar-kenzes?*"

"Yes, it must be. Bear, do your people know of such a trail?"

"I have heard of it. Shorter, but dangerous. Is this the one?"

"It *must* be," insisted Woodchuck. "If we go northeast from here, somewhere we must meet the *Ar-kenzes.*"

"But how far?" Lean Bear wondered. "The main trail takes more than a moon. And, is there water?"

"Blue Corn said the rivers run upside down."

"Yes, we know of such streams. There is water, but we must dig for it."

The two erstwhile Frenchmen looked at each other.

"If it was not usable, there would be no trail, Woodchuck," Turkey Foot pointed out.

"True. Can we do it?" Woodchuck inquired of Sky-Eyes, in French.

"It is better than fighting our countrymen," the other returned in the same tongue.

Woodchuck smiled.

"Especially since they outnumber us?" he asked, also in French.

Then he turned to Lean Bear.

"Would they not see our tracks and know where we have gone?"

"We can hide our tracks," Lean Bear advised. "Turkey Foot is skilled in such things. But we must hurry. They are not far behind."

They organized quickly, acting on the suggestions of Turkey Foot. The party split in two, with Red Feather, Moonflower, and Turkey Foot following the desert route, while the others continued toward the mountain pass.

"Wander around some," Turkey Foot advised the main party. "Move off the trail to ride as wolves a while, then back to the trail. Some stay on the trail."

This would confuse the tracks, he explained. It would be hard to tell how many horses were in the party, with all the coming and going.

"I will catch up to you," he said as they parted.

He stayed with the young couple, riding in single file, only until they were well out of sight of the main trail. He then dismounted to cut a large juniper bush growing in the rocks. Tying a rawhide pack rope to the bush, he rode slowly back along the trail, dragging the bush over the freshly made tracks.

"Go on, just follow the trail," he called back.

When he approached the main trail once again, he dismounted and carefully brushed out all tracks on the desert path, within a long bow-shot. He then remounted, carrying the juniper, until he reached a brushy ravine, where he tossed it away.

Now he hurried after the main party, pleased to note the wandering, erratic pattern of their horses' tracks. He moved erratically himself, pulling the horse off the trail sometimes, changing from walk to trot in aimless sequence. Only in rocky areas, hard to track, did he occasionally push the horse into a lope.

It was past mid morning when he overtook the others. Now, they could begin the final deception. When they came to a rocky shelf along the rim of a gully, Turkey Foot called a brief halt.

"Bear, you go east along the rocks. Try not to make tracks as long as you can. You will find their trail."

One by one, the others left the trail at different points, partially concealing their tracks when opportunity offered. Finally there were only Woodchuck, Turkey Foot, and the pack animals.

"Which are the two poorest horses?" Turkey Foot asked. "The ones without packs?"

Woodchuck nodded.

"You wish to leave them?"

"It would be best. Our back trail should now look like a band of wild horses passed through. If we turn loose a couple, it will look more so," Turkey Foot advised.

"Good. Yes, they will stay where there is browse."

"Now, when we come to the rocks ahead," Turkey Foot pointed, "you take a pack horse and do as the others. I will follow later."

It was a good plan, Woodchuck thought as he picked his way across the gravelly slope. Such a complicated and confused trail would be very difficult for their pursuers to unravel. With luck, they might not even reason out the deception. The leaving of the two pack horses was an ideal touch. If anyone had been really tracking the hoofprints they had made today, the presence of two loose horses would probably give a final impression of wandering wild horses. Turkey Foot was certainly shrewd to have thought it all out. Even if those who followed them did decipher the tracks and the little-known Desert Trail, it would take time. This would lose the pursuers at least a day's travel. And ideally, if they did not know of the Desert Trail, it would appear to them that they had mistakenly followed a band of wild horses, which had now split up in the foothills.

Woodchuck rode eastward and by mid afternoon encountered the trail of the others of the party. Still, it was nearly dusk when he came upon their night camp. It would be a fireless camp, but there was a small stream bed with puddles scattered along like beads on a thong.

Lean Bear had already urged everyone to drink as much water as possible, and to water all the horses now as well as later.

"We may not see water tomorrow," he warned. "We will fill all the water skins in the morning."

Turkey Foot did not join them until sometime after dark. He approached so silently that Woodchuck, who had taken the first watch again, was startled.

"I have watched them," Turkey Foot reported. "They seemed not to notice this trail as they passed. We will see tomorrow."

It appeared that the plan was going well. Turkey Foot slid down from his horse and squatted beside Woodchuck.

"Woodchuck, is the man Weasel a good friend?"

"Of course. Why?"

"It is nothing, maybe. He is with them."

"Yes, he is their scout, their wolf."

"They have no other tracker?"

"No. Only Pretty Weasel."

"Woodchuck, you know that this plan depends on him?"

"What do you mean?"

"Well, he is a good tracker. I saw this when we searched for your son."

"Yes, but you said they have passed the fork in the trail?"

"Yes, they have. But, Woodchuck, you know a tracker will see something wrong. A poor tracker, even, if he pays attention. The tracks that we left change there at the place where we camped. Before that, it was a party traveling with riding horses and pack horses. Suddenly, next morning . . . they saw our camp, of course . . . suddenly they are following a scatter of horses that wander. It was the best we could do, but a good tracker will see something wrong at once."

"Yes, go on."

"Well . . . I do not know . . . when they come to where there are no more tracks, Pretty Weasel will see what we have done, I think. If they are really hunting us, he could bring them back, or . . ."

"He would not do that, Turkey Foot."

"But, if any others notice, he would have to say so, too, unless he wished to trick them."

Finally, Woodchuck saw the point that Turkey Foot was trying to make. Weasel was in a very uncomfortable position. He must deliberately try to mislead his employer. Woodchuck regretted placing his friend in such a situation, but what could he have done? He did not now feel as confident as he had earlier.

"So, do you trust him?" Turkey Foot asked bluntly.

He had been asked that before, and again Woodchuck was offended by the question.

"Yes, I do," he retorted crisply.

But in the back of his mind was a gnawing doubt. After all, his life, the lives of them all, were in the hands of this man, Pretty Weasel. Despite the fact that the two of them had owed each other their lives, that had been long ago. Even then, he had known Weasel for only a few weeks before they parted. And again, for three days in Santa Fe, some ten or twelve years later.

With some alarm, he realized that he did not really know Pretty Weasel at all. Of course, he trusted him, but how far? Sometime, somewhere, would there come a situation where Weasel would be forced to say, enough, I cannot do any more for friendship? Where was that point of turning?

"Yes, I trust him," he said more softly.

To himself, he added, silently, another thought: because I have to trust him. We have nothing else.

# 21

>> >> >>

The next day on the Desert Trail passed without incident. Travel was little different than they had experienced on a hundred other days. The terrain, only one sleep from the main trail, was quite similar, though they knew that would soon change.

One major difference, of course, was the threat of pursuit. Lean Bear and Woodchuck brought up the rear, and from time to time rode back to watch for any sign of activity on the back trail. They saw nothing, and through that day and the next, became more pleased at the apparent success of their strategy. By the third day, it seemed that only routine watch was needed to protect the rear of the column.

Attention turned now to the trail ahead. They had very little idea as to how long the Desert Trail might be, or when they could expect to reach the *Ar-kenzes*, or at what point. Sky-Eyes, familiar with maps and charts from his formal military training, attempted to sketch his impression of the trail in the sand. He was only guessing, but his best estimate said that it would be at least two weeks, half a moon, before they reached the river and familiar territory. That guess was based on their ability to travel well and keep moving.

At the other, longer end of possible days required, the outlook became quite gloomy. If they had trouble finding water, if any of the horses became lame or unable to travel, any of the unexpected occurrences of the trail . . . well, estimates then would range up to a moon or longer. If at all. That was a reality that they hated to consider, but one that must be faced, as they discussed the possibilities.

Sky-Eyes, Woodchuck, and Lean Bear had drawn aside a little way to discuss the situation without alarming the young couple. Red Feather and Moonflower, however, were basically so preoccupied with each other that they noticed little else.

"How long do you think, Bear, until we reach the river?" Sky-Eyes asked.

Lean Bear shrugged.

"Who knows? When we get there, we are there."

This attitude on the part of the people of the plains was one of the most frustrating for their adopted sons.

Woodchuck sighed. His wife's people lived one day at a time. Lived it hard, enthusiastically, joyfully, and thankfully. But just one day at a time. Let tomorrow take care of itself. There was planning of a sort, of course. The preparation for winter, the hunting of buffalo for that purpose. But even that was largely unplanned. The hunt would take place when the buffalo came. Why be concerned about it until then?

His concern for the future amused his wife.

"If there is nothing you can do to change it, why worry about it?" Yellow Head once asked him. "Who knows what may happen by then?"

This philosophy was reflected again in Lean Bear's remark.

"When we get there, we are there."

By the third day, water was becoming scarce. When they stopped that evening, it was necessary to dig deep into the sand to obtain enough to slake their thirst and that of the horses. Even that was a slow process, waiting until the sandy basin filled.

Through the night, one or another of the members of the party kept watch at the seep-well, drinking, filling water skins, or watering the horses. They were moving again by the time Sun Boy raised his torch above Earth's rim.

Even so, the blistering heat began to take its toll by midday. The horses plodded on without energy, placing one foot in front of another, stumbling and not caring. After a halt to rest and sip meagerly from their water supply, they moved on, walking and leading the horses now.

Evening was still some distance away when they stopped for the night. Turkey Foot and Woodchuck began to dig for water while the others rigged makeshift shade with some of their robes and blankets.

"We need some poles," Lean Bear announced.

The others chuckled. They had seen no growth that even resembled a pole for two days. There was scarcely enough browse for the horses.

One concern was whether they were actually following the right trail. In many places there seemed no trail at all, across some stretch of blowing sand. Then they would encounter a rutted slope which allowed them to reorient their course, following the footsteps of generations long gone. Woodchuck wondered who had been the first to attempt this crossing, when the land was young. More to the point, the first to attempt it and live to say yes, there is a trail, a way to get across.

And why? *Why* had that figure from the dim and misty past chosen to risk his life to follow an obscure game trail? Had he been lost, and taken the wrong path? Was he a hunter, following his quarry into unknown territory? Or was *he* the quarry, pursued by wild animals which had become the hunters? Yet another idea suggested that the first pathfinder might have been pursued, like themselves, by two-legged hunters, a force stronger than himself. It might have been less dangerous to try to cross the desert than to face the danger that threatened behind.

He wondered about that, too. Had the French party really turned back, or lost the trail, as they hoped? The longer he thought, the more improbable it seemed that they would simply give up the chase. He thought about

Pretty Weasel, and wondered again how far Weasel would go, how far he *could* go, to protect the fugitives. Weasel's own safety might be at stake. Unpleasant things could happen to a guide who misled his employer, even accidently. And intentionally, *aiee!* Once again, he reminded himself that Weasel, experienced in tracking, must know what had happened to the party they sought. Their safety would depend on his actions.

But for now, the risk was not from those who followed, but from the elements. Water supply was questionable, even in this camp, and what about tomorrow, and the next day, and the one after that? Their rate of travel was poor. They had covered perhaps half the desired distance today. It was hard to estimate, of course, with few landmarks, and a desperate sameness. Sometimes, as he plodded along that afternoon, Woodchuck had felt that the heat and the blinding sun were affecting his mind. Maybe he was already dead, and doomed by his past sins to wander forever on this trail that led through a blistering hell.

He looked over at the young couple, who appeared tired, but happy, totally absorbed in each other. Ah, the resiliency of youth, he sighed. He wondered if they realized the seriousness of their situation.

"Bear, could we travel at night?" he asked. "It would be cooler, and we could rest during the heat of day."

"We *could,*" agreed Lean Bear, "but we do not know the trail. We could become lost very easily."

"But we could follow the stars."

"Yes. But does the trail go straight, or bend sometimes, like most trails? We must not lose it."

A compromise was considered, to rest during the heat of the day and travel hard in the cooler morning and evening hours, sleeping when it became too dark to travel. They quickly realized, however, that it would be impractical. They could not travel until full dark, and then look for a place to camp and to dig for water.

No, they could only continue as they were, making just a half day's distance each day, hoping for water at day's end, and spending a restless night wondering about pursuit.

He found himself unable to follow the easygoing philosophy of Lean Bear. He could tell himself it was the best way, but he was not convinced. The situation was far too critical for him to relax. Still, he retained hope. Maybe tomorrow they would find water more available. He visualized a cool, crystal-clear stream, back in the tall-grass hills, the Sacred Hills of the People. There would be shade, and grass for the horses, and safety in which to rest.

It was doubly depressing, then, when the next evening they dug deep into the stream bed, to find . . . nothing. There was only more sand. It was damp, but there was no seep of water, even after an evening of patient waiting. Only damp sand.

# 22

>> >> >>

"There is no trouble!" Lean Bear insisted. "We have water in our water skins."

"But what about the horses?" Sky-Eyes demanded.

Lean Bear shrugged.

"We give them a little. Tomorrow maybe we find some more water."

"Bear," the other snapped angrily, "you know each camp has been drier than the last, since we left the trail. Why should we think that there is water ahead?"

Lean Bear pointed to the traces of travel, a path angling toward the dry stream bed and then up the slope on the other side.

"Because others have traveled this way. Sky-Eyes, a trail does not just go nowhere and then stop. It comes out the other side."

The logic seemed reasonable, they had to admit. The concern of Sky-Eyes and Woodchuck was for the season. In this country, a trail might be acceptable, even easy and good at one season, but treacherous and deadly at another. This was the dry portion of summer, in a year that began to appear drier than some. The Moon of Thunder, July by the calendar of their motherland, was gone. The summer storms which rumbled across the plains, bringing refreshing relief and moisture along with the violence of Rain Maker's thunderous drum and his spears of real-fire, were in the past now. It was August, Woodchuck

115

thought, the time of the Red Moon. Red, because the coppery fire of Sun Boy's torch reached its hottest at this time. It rose to blistering extremes before starting to flicker and grow cold and yellow in the moons ahead, almost dying in the Moon of Long Nights. Woodchuck feared that the timing of this trek across the Desert Trail was all wrong.

"Maybe we should go back," he suggested.

"To Santa Fe?" asked the astonished Lean Bear.

"No, only to the main trail."

"Woodchuck, that would lose half a moon!"

"But there is water, and we know the way. It seems we are not followed now."

"*Aiee!* We are halfway to the *Ar-kenzes!*" protested Lean Bear. "Would you lose that much travel?"

"If we must," Woodchuck said stubbornly. "At least, we know we would have water tomorrow night."

Lean Bear threw up his hands in consternation, and gave a frustrated sigh.

"I will never understand your ways, Woodchuck. Your tribe must have been much different from your wife's."

Sky-Eyes intervened.

"It does no good to argue, my friends. We could do it either way. Let us have a council, and decide."

It was usual to have a fire for council, but there was no ready supply of fuel. They gathered in a circle, and Sky-Eyes, as leader of the party, began the discussion. He repeated the dilemma, as it had just been argued by Woodchuck and Lean Bear.

"So," he finished, "we go on, or go back. How do you say? Turkey Foot?"

"I say, go on. Each day brings us closer."

"Woodchuck?"

"Go back," Woodchuck said uncomfortably. "It is safer."

"Lean Bear?"

"Our people know this country, Sky-Eyes. Not here, but lands with this spirit. I say with Turkey Foot. Go on. We will find a way."

"Red Feather?"

The young man looked startled. His opinion had never been asked in council.

"I would let my wife speak first," he said, embarrassed.

"Does she understand the choice we have?" Sky-Eyes inquired.

"Yes. We have talked of it. Sign talk. She knows the danger."

Sky-Eyes turned to the girl.

"What is your say?" he signed.

Moonflower's eyes opened wide with astonishment.

"*I* have a say?"

"Of course. You are now of the People."

"But . . ." she paused, confused. "Women do not speak in council," she signed.

"Our women do," Red Feather told her.

"I do not know," the girl signed. "I will say as my husband says."

Red Feather smiled.

"I say go on."

Sky-Eyes sat for a moment. There was no point now in voicing an opinion. The decision was already made.

"Then we go on. Bear, Turkey Foot, you will tell us what we must do?"

"Yes, of course."

"Then, how do we give horses water from water skins?"

"I will show you," smiled Turkey Foot.

He selected an area of soft sand and scooped a shallow depression with his hands. Then he took his buffalo robe, and spread it over the hole, skin side up, pressing the robe into the hole as a lining.

"It is like a cooking pit!" observed Red Feather.

Turkey Foot nodded. He led his horse to the skin, and carefully poured a little water into the depression. The horse sucked noisily, and licked at the remaining moisture.

"That will be enough," Turkey Foot observed. "Bring another one."

One by one, the horses received a tiny ration of water. The humans, too, wet their mouths and cracked lips, and wished for more, but dared not drink more. Their thirst would cool, perhaps, with the night, and then tomorrow, in the heat of day, their scanty water supply would be used to better effect.

Woodchuck sought out Lean Bear, as the lengthening shadows darkened into twilight.

"What happens, Bear, if we do *not* find water in a day or two?"

He dreaded the answer.

"It is no matter," Lean Bear said casually. "We kill one of the horses. Drink its blood. That keeps us going for another day."

Woodchuck had eaten raw liver in the spring, at the time of the first buffalo kill, since he became one of the People. Although he had been repulsed at first, he had found that there was an invigorating effect. It had become almost a craving, that deep-seated urgency for the nutrients in the fresh, warm liver, after a winter of dried meat and pemmican. But, to drink blood? However, even that was not the main question.

"What about the *next* day?"

Lean Bear looked around their makeshift camp.

"*Aiee!*" he exclaimed, as if he saw no problem. "We have *eight* horses."

Eight horses, thought Woodchuck. Eight days. If they had not found water by that time, they would be on foot, in addition to dying of thirst. Ah, well, he thought, maybe it will turn out well. The others seemed to have no excessive concern. Even Sky-Eyes appeared willing to let things happen as they would. He smiled to himself. There had been a time when he had started across country to return to the People, alone, on foot, through unknown territory, armed only with a bow and a knife. Maybe he was getting old. No, that was not it. His concern, he decided, was not for himself so much as for his son, Red Feather, and his new bride.

He looked over at Moonflower, her dark beauty somewhat jaded by the hard day. She still displayed a strength and an inner beauty that he knew would be admired by the People. He was proud of his son's choice, and was certain that Yellow Head, too, would approve.

Yes, he worried for them, he had to admit, for the young couple just beginning their life together. He wanted it to be easy for them, better than it had been for him. But already . . . maybe that was just never to be. We suffer for our children, he supposed, hoping they will have it better. It seemed not to bother them, however, so he finally gave up trying to figure out the way of things.

"I will take the first watch," he offered.

The others nodded.

"I will follow you, Woodchuck," Turkey Foot called. "You will have to wake me."

Because there was no water, Woodchuck knew. Under usual circumstances, Turkey Foot would drink all the water he could hold, just before retiring. His full bladder would waken him halfway through the night, to take the watch.

But tonight, he would have to be wakened. There was no water.

# 23

>> >> >>

As they started to travel next morning, Lean Bear showed the others a custom of his people to help avoid the tortures of thirst. He selected a small, smooth stone from the dry stream bed. It was rounded by eons of tumbling and polishing during seasons when the stream flowed. In size, it resembled the ball of a man's thumb, and was somewhat flattened.

"Its medicine is that of the water," he explained. "It has been rolled by water since long-ago times, maybe all the way from the mountains. The spirit of the water is in it, and it makes water to rise up in your mouth."

He popped the stone into his mouth. Turkey Foot had already selected his stone, and the others hastened to follow the example. Woodchuck was surprised to find that there was a noticeable effect. The presence of something in the mouth seemed to stimulate the flow of saliva. In addition, as they traveled, he found that with his mouth closed over the stone, there was less drying of the delicate inner surfaces. His tongue remained moist, and was less swollen than on the day before.

Even so, as the day began to swelter under the merciless heat of Sun Boy's torch, nothing seemed to help any longer. The shimmering waves of heat distorted the vision, giving the appearance of rivers and lakes of cool water. Once it was so real that Woodchuck actually believed it. He raised his arm to point, but could not bring sound to his parched lips. Before he could muster the energy to clear his throat and speak, the vision was gone. A chance variation, a random shift in the direction of the air currents, had destroyed something good and lovely.

He wondered if he was losing his mind. He began to think that the spirit of the place was an enemy. Not passively, but aggressively an enemy, quietly plotting the destruction of them all. Maybe, as the People believed, there are places whose spirit is good or evil. The Sacred Hills exuded a good feeling, a beneficial spirit. Could it not be that this place was basically evil and malevolent, striving to kill them?

By mid morning, he was sure of it. They encountered a puddle of water, several paces across, and urged their horses toward it.

"Wait!" warned Lean Bear. "Do not let them drink yet."

He dismounted and handed his rein to Turkey Foot to hold while he walked toward the pool. At the edge, he squatted and dipped a cupped palm into the water. Tasting cautiously, he then shook his hand to dry it, and turned his head to spit as he rose to his feet.

"Bad water," he said simply. "Bad medicine. Let no one drink."

Woodchuck stared at the inviting pool. At first glance, it seemed the answer to survival. Then, as he studied the pool in a new light, he began to notice telltale signs. A source of water this size should have been an oasis of green. It should be ringed with willows, perhaps a large cottonwood or two, and grass should flourish on its banks. There should be game trails leading to the water hole.

He saw none of these things. The only vegetation consisted of a few wisps of scrubby sedge sprouting from the cracked mud. There were no game trails. Around the edge of the water was a whitish crust of alkali, which had escaped his notice before. This was not a spring, then, or even a puddle in an otherwise dry creek bed. He could see now that the ground sloped slightly upward in all directions for a little way. There was probably no time when the water in this basin was ever running water. It was stagnant, concentrating the alkali through the years, with no opportunity to cleanse itself by a thorough washing of fresh water.

Lean Bear expressed the same thought somewhat differently as they reined away.

"Dead water. There is no life in it. Bad medicine."

In his heat-fogged mind, Woodchuck began to think of this as a trap. The desert, or its spirit, was planning evil for them. Planning to kill them. The alkali pool was a trap, a cruel and taunting trap. To kill them outright would be simple, but here was an opportunity to torture them, taunt them with the promise of water, only to dash their hopes. Yes, the spirit of this place must be evil.

"We should lead the horses," Sky-Eyes advised.

They dismounted and plodded on, the horses plodding hopelessly behind.

They paused at midday for a rest in what makeshift shade they could contrive, and moved on to another dry camp in the evening. They discussed the details of sacrificing the horse for life-giving moisture.

"We will do it in the morning, to give strength for the day," Lean Bear advised. "That gray pack horse, you think?"

The others agreed. The gray was showing signs of faltering already.

"What about its packs?" asked Turkey Foot.

"Divide the load between others," suggested Sky-Eyes. "We will walk, to save the horses."

He paused a moment.

"We could leave part of our packs behind."

"Not yet, Sky-Eyes. We are still moving," spoke Lean Bear. "Maybe later."

The camp was depressing that evening. Dry, hungry, without even the cheer of a night fire. Turkey Foot finally helped at least the latter circumstance, out of sheer boredom. He found a dead bush a little way into the desert, and broke an armful of dry branches to carry to the center of their camp. Skillfully, he built his small pile of twigs, and then drew forth his fire-sticks. In a short while a bright little fire was crackling.

"There!" announced Turkey Foot proudly.

There was nothing to cook, and the fire was not needed for warmth, but somehow, everyone seemed to feel better. It was a declaration, a ritual, that went with the making of a camp, however temporary. Turkey Foot's simple one-word statement spoke much more. Here I will camp, it said, an announcement to whatever spirits might inhabit this strange territory. Not in a sense of defiance, but an announcement that this is the way it is. In a sense, the establishment of a fire might be seen as asking permission from the resident spirits to come into their territory.

Woodchuck remembered that he had once seen Pale Star place a tiny piece of dried meat on a new campfire. It was a custom, she said, practiced by Traveler, the roving trader who had taught her as she grew up. He had always made such a sacrifice when he entered new territory, Star had said.

Thoughtfully, Woodchuck rose and took a tiny pinch of tobacco from his pouch. He knelt and placed it on the fire.

"It is good, Woodchuck," Lean Bear said approvingly.

"Anyway, it can hurt nothing," Woodchuck mumbled, a little embarrassed.

He glanced over at Sky-Eyes. That individual was gazing into the fire, lost in thought, and seemed to notice nothing unusual in the symbolic offering to appease the gods of the desert. They had both come a long way since they left France, reflected Woodchuck.

"I will take the first watch," announced Red Feather.

Woodchuck started to protest, but thought better of it. If his son felt strong enough, let him take his turn. It would build his strength and confidence. There was little danger here, anyway.

As if to instill confidence, a coyote called from somewhere in the distance, and another answered. That was a most encouraging sound. At least, if there were coyotes, there must be enough life in this wretched desert to sustain their needs.

The fire was dying as Red Feather picked up his bow and walked a little way out of camp. Woodchuck sought his sleeping robe. He lay awake a long time, the problems of the party whirling in his head. What a strange journey this had been. He finally fell asleep, marveling at a trading venture which had actually been quite routine for the past few years. It had this time become a thing of surprises, of new experiences, of hidden dangers. At least, Red Feather was alive, and had come to manhood . . . a wife . . .

He woke with a start. Red Feather, on watch, was shouting for help. The others were leaping up from their robes, seizing weapons. Woodchuck grabbed his belt-ax and sprinted after the others in the dim starlight. He heard Moonflower calling her husband's name.

A scuffling flurry of activity was taking place where the sentry post had been. He gripped the ax and ran forward. Red Feather and another man . . . Turkey Foot, it now seemed . . . were wrestling with a large buck antelope in its dying struggles. The feathered shaft of an arrow jutted from the creature's rib cage.

The struggles were weakening now. Turkey Foot looked up.

"Is everyone here?" he asked cheerfully. "I will open a vein, and each one can drink a little blood."

He drew his knife, and the others gathered. Woodchuck was surprised to find that he was not only willing, but eager, to participate.

"We can save the gray horse till later," Turkey Foot joked as he carefully slit the jugular vein.

He held his thumb on the wound and motioned to Moonflower.

"Go ahead, little one."

The girl dropped to her knees without hesitation, and bent over the still-quivering carcass. Turkey Foot smiled up at Woodchuck.

"Our camp fire worked, my friend."

# 24

>> >> >>

They gorged themselves on the life-giving fluids of the antelope. The animal had simply wandered up to Red Feather's post and watched him curiously until he shot it. First the blood, then the liver, and finally they chewed the moisture from the meat.

Lean Bear opened the stomach to utilize the fluid in the greenish slime contained in the paunch. No one else felt inclined to share that experience. Their initial craving for moisture had been somewhat sated by the blood.

They were still greedily sucking the juices from the flesh when day began to dawn. It was time to move, while they were still refreshed from the kill. Oddly, Woodchuck felt that he could understand how it must feel to be a wolf. There was little difference, he noted. The party had dragged down the antelope, as a wolf pack might, and had gone through the feeding frenzy of the animal side of their nature. It was a little disconcerting to realize that they were no farther than this from the predators. There could be one difference, though.

He motioned to Red Feather, and they carried the head of the antelope aside and propped it up. Woodchuck stood formally before it.

"My brother, we are sorry to kill you," he said solemnly, "but you are our life. Without you, we die."

They backed away, very formally.

"Is this always done, Woodchuck?" asked Moonflower in Spanish.

"No, not every time. The first buffalo kill of the season. A special kill, like a white buffalo. Or, like this. It is medicine."

"What were the words that you say?"

"Something like our medicine man would say. 'We are sorry to kill you, but we must do so to live.' The buffalo eat grass, we eat the buffalo. Somewhere we must say thank-you."

He was a little embarrassed, not quite certain how he did feel about it, or why he felt that it was appropriate. He only felt that it was important, though he did not entirely understand. However, this did not seem to bother Moonflower. She smiled broadly.

"It is good," she observed in sign talk. "I like this custom."

Dawn was growing now. Lean Bear suggested that they use most of what water they had left to give to the horses.

"We may find water," he observed cheerfully. "This antelope did."

It was true, Woodchuck reflected. Even though the antelope was a creature of the dry country, it must drink occasionally. Somewhere, within a day's travel, there was water. It might be only a puddle in a creek bed, or a sweet clear spring, but it was somewhere.

"Should we search for water, or travel on?" Sky-Eyes asked.

"Keep on the trail," advised Lean Bear. "People have used this trail for many seasons. It will lead *to* the water, not away from it."

Woodchuck began to understand. A trail, any trail across open country, would follow from one camping place to another. He had noticed this on the main Southwest Trail. At intervals of a day's journey, travelers must camp for the night. They would seek out the best places. Those who followed in later days or years would have the same needs and would seek out the same places to spend the night. Campsites with water, relative security from surprise attack, and of course, at approximately a day's travel from the previous camp.

In the grass country of the People, there were a number of sites known as "the camping place." They were spaced along the ancient trails, spaced at convenient distances like beads on a thong. The ashes and charcoal of yesterday's fire might rest on those of last year. In turn, those covered the long-dead fires of people and tribes whose trails led back into the misty past. Back to Creation, maybe, Looks Far had once told him.

Lean Bear had been assuming, apparently, that the same was true here. At intervals of a day's travel, there should be campsites. Because of the season, many were dry, but some should have available water, even though they might have to dig for it. The antelope was a good sign. Its presence meant that there was water somewhere. Lean Bear, with his optimism that seemed foolish at times, was actually seeing the situation with realism and clarity. All things considered, it now seemed entirely likely that a day's journey ahead of them in the direction they were traveling there would be water.

"Let us move!" Lean Bear called.

They set out, the morning still comfortably mild, leading the thirsty horses and walking as fast as they comfortably could. By the time they stopped to rest in the heat of midday, their optimism was ebbing rapidly. The horses walked among dry brush and drier sand, dejectedly poking around for some chance mouthful of nutrition or moisture. A couple of the weaker animals stood listlessly, too far gone to have any interest. Woodchuck watched the gray, wondering if it could survive the afternoon's travel. He wondered if the expected campsite with water might be a day's travel for someone in good condition, traveling well at a favorable time of the season. They were certainly not able to accomplish such a distance. They might fall short of the water on which their lives would soon depend.

After a shorter rest than usual, they moved on. One foot forward, then the other, a step at a time, weakness dragging them down with each stride. Woodchuck noticed that he was no longer sweating. His body was too dry to give up any of its moisture. The scant amount furnished by the antelope was now gone. His lips and tongue were swollen and cracked, completely lacking the flow of saliva. He continued to plod along, wondering how the others were doing. He felt physically unable to look, more than an occasional glance. His muscles ached so badly that it was all he could do to concentrate on placing one foot in front of the other.

Shimmering mirages danced ahead of them on the trail, taunting and tempting with the promise of cool water that was not there. The lake would ripple and beckon, and then, with a shifting of the hot desert breeze, would vanish before their eyes. The vision was so real, sometimes, that Woodchuck was certain that this time . . . then it would vanish, dashing his hopes once more into the blistering sand under his feet.

Sometimes, even, the mirage was so detailed that it seemed he could see the banks of the lake or stream, the grassy slopes and the trees that grew along the shores. He was looking at such a particularly inviting scene when the vision shimmered and disappeared. He sighed and started to look down at his plodding feet again, but something made him glance up once more.

The vision of water was gone, blown aside by a treacherous shift of the air. But a part of the vision was still there. In the earth tones of brown and yellow, there was unmistakably something green. Woodchuck managed to raise an arm and point ahead.

"Look!" he croaked hoarsely.

A fringe of scrubby willows straggled along the winding course of a waterway ahead. Where there were willows, there must be water, even if they had to dig for it. They stumbled forward at a quicker pace.

Suddenly, one of the horses raised its head and nickered softly, peering ahead with interest. It had scented water. Another animal lifted its ears and shuffled forward into a tired trot. In a few moments, the entire party, horses and people, were stumbling across the flat toward the willows.

Woodchuck could smell it now, the moldy odor of wet soil and growing things, a smell like that of early spring, in the Moon of Awakening. He could see the loose horses splashing into the water and beginning to drink.

"Drink slowly!" Lean Bear warned, as he dropped flat to plunge his face into the water.

# 25

>> >> >>

They remained at the water hole, not only through the night, but all of the next day. Their dried and parchment-like skin began to regain supple elasticity. Sunken eyes became bright and alert. Cracked lips and swollen tongues returned to normal.

The change in the horses was equally remarkable. By the time darkness fell, on their first night there, they could see the animals responding. The plodding, stumbling oblivion was replaced by an interest in the world. Even the gray pack horse revived and began to forage along the creek bed, browsing on the vegetation that moisture allowed to grow there.

At dawn, Woodchuck and Turkey Foot took their bows and hunted up and down the stream. They had some dried meat left, but the possibility of fresh meat, properly cooked, would be a welcome change. They hoped for another antelope. It had been impractical to carry meat from Red Feather's kill in the blistering heat. The dangers of eating spoiled meat were well known. With regret, they had left what remains there were to the scavengers of the desert. Now, another kill would bring the whole party to good physical condition. The quiet dejection of the day before was already being replaced by cheerful optimism.

The hunters found no large game, though there were tracks along the water's edge. Turkey Foot pointed to the tracks of a large antelope, perhaps a day old, in the drying mud.

"Red Feather's buck," he announced.

Woodchuck was not certain whether the other was joking, or expressing a serious opinion. It was hard to tell, with Turkey Foot's serious demeanor, balanced by his droll sense of humor.

At any rate, they saw no antelope. That would most likely be the only large game in this area. Deer, elk, or buffalo would seek out better grazing, in areas of heavier vegetation. Even so, they managed to shoot a couple of long-legged desert rabbits. Since the party had been virtually dying only a day ago, even that good fortune seemed a bright and promising omen.

They lounged around the camp, sleeping, rising to drink again, or walking lazily along the stream bed. It was apparent to all that the worst of the journey was behind them.

"How far to the river now?" asked Woodchuck.

Lean Bear shrugged in his quizzical way. He did not even speak until he had finished polishing the rabbit leg bone he was gnawing. Finally he tossed the bone aside, wiped his fingers on his leggings, and belched comfortably.

"I still do not know, Woodchuck. But, we are many sleeps closer than we were."

The others laughed, and it was a comfortable, pleasant sound, which had not been heard at their camps for many days. They watched the horses, now playful in their newfound strength. The animals were rolling in an open flat beside the water, stretching and scratching their withers on the ground, then rolling to scratch the other side. Finally they would rise and shake briskly, shedding any sand and debris in a cloud of dust.

Moonflower was fascinated. Her experience with horses was quite limited.

"Why do they roll?" she asked her husband, using sign talk.

"Who knows? To scratch, maybe. The worth of a horse can be told by how many rolls."

Moonflower looked at him skeptically.

"Really. It is true," Red Feather insisted. "A very fine horse rolls many times, a poor horse only once or twice, or only on one side."

The girl was skeptical. She looked over at her husband's father, who sat smiling in amusement at the sign talk conversation.

"Is that true?" she asked him.

"Yes, little one, it is true. A horse that is strong rolls many times from side to side. Maybe five or six, even more. A weak horse does not care."

Moonflower was still unconvinced that they were serious, and not merely teasing her. Yet, she knew that Woodchuck was a kind man, and would probably not continue such a deception. If it had been Turkey Foot, whose droll humor often turned to practical jokes, she might never have believed it.

They prepared to settle down for the night, confident and comfortable for the first time since they had left the main trail. Dusk was deepening, and the sounds of the evening indicated that the creatures of the night were coming alive.

"Sun Boy chooses his paint well tonight," said Red Feather appreciatively.

Woodchuck smiled. He had heard Yellow Head make such a statement many times as they watched a prairie sunset.

Maybe it was their preoccupation with the beauty of the western sky that made them careless. They had just survived a close brush with death, and it was easy to assume that all was well now. Their first indication to the contrary was a soft nicker from one of the horses. Turkey Foot rose to his feet to investigate.

The other animals had stopped grazing now, and were facing northeast, ears pricked forward in anticipation. A dozen men were riding into the camp. They wore buckskin leggings, and were naked from the waist up, except for a war shirt of some sort worn by one who appeared to be the leader. They stopped a few paces away and sat quietly on their horses, alert and suspicious.

Woodchuck quickly assessed the situation. The men were well armed, and their demeanor said plainly that they were in control of the situation. He did not recognize their tribe. The style of their hair, the cut of their leggings and moccasins were unfamiliar to him. The strangers had a distinct advantage if conflict erupted. Their weapons were already in their hands, while those in the camp were laid aside.

Sky-Eyes was rising to his feet, slowly and cautiously, with his right hand raised, palm forward in the sign for friendly greeting.

"I am not armed," it indicated to the newcomers.

Sky-Eyes would be the one to speak for the group. Not only was he the leader of this mission, but the most experienced in dealing with unknown tribes. He had learned much from Pale Star since they had been together. Both men had marveled at Star's ability to begin trade with an unknown tribe. She had learned this as a child, and was always quick to take the initiative. This technique would be necessary here.

"Welcome to our camp, my brothers," Sky-Eyes signed.

The chief on the bay horse glared at him.

"Who are you? Why are you in our territory?"

"We are only passing through, my chief," Sky-Eyes signed casually. "We are traders."

"What is your tribe?"

"I am Sky-Eyes, of the Elk-dog People."

He omitted mention of the fact that Lean Bear and Turkey Foot were of another tribe. If the strangers called this their territory, their range might adjoin that of the Head Splitters. There was no way of knowing whether their contacts were friendly or warlike. The newcomer, as if in answer to this thought, pointed to Turkey Foot.

"You lie," he signed. "That one is a Head Splitter. That one, too." He indicated Lean Bear. "Now, who are you?"

Sky-Eyes smiled casually.

"Your eyes are good, my chief. These are Head Splitters. They are sometimes our allies. We have been to Santa Fe together, to trade with the Spanish."

In a quiet aside, he tossed a quick question to Lean Bear.

"Who are they?"

"We know this tribe," Bear answered cautiously. "We fight them sometimes. Just now we are at peace."

Sky-Eyes plunged ahead.

"We have gifts," he signed. "I will get them from the pack."

He strode over to the packs, more confidently than he actually felt, watched closely by the warriors. He opened one of the rawhide bags and drew out four knives. Medicine knives, they had been called when the first ones were seen. The difference between steel implements and the flint knives in common use was so striking that they were considered supernatural. This had formed the basis for their original trading venture. It was to be hoped that this unknown tribe still held respect for the medicine of the metal tools.

Sky-Eyes walked back and handed the knives to the leader.

"Medicine knives," he signed. "We have many more things to trade, if your tribe wishes. How are you called, my chief?"

It was apparent that the strangers were impressed by the gifts. They began to relax a little.

"I am White Wolf," their leader signed. "How is it we do not know you? Have you been here before?"

"Not here. We are from the tallgrass country. We use the Southwest Trail. This time, we come back by the Desert Trail."

The other nodded, apparently satisfied. He dismounted, speaking to the others, who also swung down.

"We will camp here," he signed. "You will tell us about this trading. You can get more weapons like these knives?"

Woodchuck took a deep breath of relief. The dangerous confrontation was past.

# 26
>> >> >>

**A**s it turned out, the chance encounter proved beneficial to the traders. The hunting party of White Wolf had made an antelope kill earlier in the day, and they were able to exchange a few steel arrowheads and a lance point for some of the meat. Actually, it was not formal trading, but more like an exchange of gifts with newfound friends.

White Wolf seemed to realize the benefit that could result from their use of the Desert Trail across his territory.

"You will come back next year to trade?" he asked.

"Yes," Sky-Eyes assured him. "We may take the other, the Mountain Trail."

White Wolf nodded.

"Use our trail if you wish. Tell anyone you meet that White Wolf has said it."

Woodchuck was elated. With this permission, and the implied protection of White Wolf, their trading could expand. They would have access to the shorter route, and could furnish trade goods to this new tribe.

"Where are your people, my chief?" he signed, as they sat around the fire.

"They move camp, as yours do," White Wolf answered. "This season, to the east of here. We go south in winter, to the canyon."

"The canyon?"

"Yes. The Canyon of Hard Wood. Bow wood."

He pointed to his weapon.

"We do not know this canyon," observed Sky-Eyes.

White Wolf nodded.

"It is south of you. We seldom go north of the river . . . the one you call *Ar-kenzes.*"

"How far to the river, from here?" asked Woodchuck.

"Maybe four sleeps. You travel well?"

"Yes. Now, we can. We were very dry until we found the water here."

"Yes," White Wolf agreed. "There are dry camps. How did you come to take the Desert Trail?"

Sky-Eyes and Woodchuck exchanged glances.

"It will do no harm to tell the truth," Sky-Eyes said quickly in French.

He began to sign.

"We were being pursued. There was a disagreement. We were outnumbered, so we took this trail. Those who followed us went on up the Mountain Trail, maybe. We have not seen them."

White Wolf nodded understandingly.

"If we see them, we will kill them for you."

This was becoming complicated. They had no desire to bring the wrath of White Wolf's tribe down on the French exploring party.

"Thank you, my chief," Woodchuck signed, "but it is not necessary. They were our friends, and will be again. This was only a thing of misunderstanding."

"Ah, yes. Politics!" White Wolf signed with a shake of his head.

"Yes," agreed Woodchuck sadly. "It hurts many friendships."

They talked in sign talk until far into the night, exchanging creation stories and tales of Long-ago Times when the world was young and animals and man spoke the same tongue.

When they parted in the morning, White Wolf made an elaborate speech in sign talk.

"It is good that we met, my brothers. Travel well . . .

may your path be easy, game plentiful, and may all your mares drop buffalo horses next season."

It was a highly satisfactory conclusion to what could have been a disastrous meeting. The two parties separated to continue their respective journeys.

It was not four sleeps, but five, before they reached the river. There was one camp where they dug for water, but it was easy, and water plentiful when the seep-hole was finished. The country became greener after that, and it was no surprise, on the day they reached the river.

It was late afternoon when Turkey Foot, acting as wolf, rode back to meet them and point ahead as they crossed a low rise.

"Look!"

Some distance ahead, a dark green stripe wound snake-like through the lighter green of the prairie grasses.

"The *Ar-kenzes!*" Turkey Foot indicated, as proudly as if he had dug its entire length himself. "I know where we are, now."

The river's wandering course, marked by the lush growth of willows and cottonwoods, stretched from one horizon to the other. It was almost lost in the blue of the distance to the east. To the west, its path was contorted by another tributary, and was finally lost behind rolling undulations of the prairie as it neared earth's rim. Directly in front of them, the river's course ran due east and west. On the other side, the Southwest Trail wandered across the sloping rise beyond the river.

Jubilant at their success, they rode to the river's edge to water the animals and to drink, themselves. Now, they were practically in their own country. No more of wondering over unknown spirits and strange lands. They could see country, on the other side, that they had seen before, the trail that they had ridden.

It was growing late, now. It would not be long until darkness fell.

"Shall we cross and camp on the other side?" asked Sky-Eyes.

"Maybe not," cautioned Lean Bear. "The sands are sometimes hungry here."

They looked at the water, hardly a stone's throw across. It rippled, gently and quietly, deceptive in its calm.

"The sands shift when rains come and water rises," Lean Bear was explaining. "What was a good crossing last season may be dangerous now."

"Dangerous? In what way, Bear?" Sky-Eyes asked. "The current is not strong."

"Not the current. The sand. Always shifting. In deep water, the horses swim. But in loose sand, it sucks at their feet, pulls them under. Best we wait until morning."

Sometime later, after they had established camp, they sat talking around the fire.

"Tomorrow we part," observed Lean Bear. "Our tribe is northwest of here this season. Yours is east."

That seemed odd. They were accustomed to returning over Raton Pass, traveling together until they were well out on the plains. Then the Head Splitters would leave the trail to join their people, while the others continued east. This time, they had reached the main trail much farther east. Tomorrow the party would split, Turkey Foot and Lean Bear to go one direction, the others the opposite way, to rejoin their respective tribes.

Woodchuck always found this parting a bit sad. Maybe a hint of the life he had left behind crept in, a twinge of regret at things that could never be again.

"We will join you at your Sun Dance next year," Lean Bear was saying. "On Sycamore Creek?"

"Yes," Sky-Eyes nodded. "Do you want to try this Desert Trail from this end next year?"

"Maybe so. It would be faster."

"And the season better," added Sky-Eyes.

"We can decide then," concluded Lean Bear. "If the season is good, who knows? We know the way, now."

"This has been a good season's trade," observed Sky-Eyes.

"It did not seem so for a while," Lean Bear stated. "*Aiee*, it was bad for Red Feather."

"But he found a wife!" Turkey Foot chuckled. "Besides, he is alive. He has very good luck!"

"Yes, and he killed the antelope that saved us," Lean Bear agreed. "His luck is very good, his medicine strong."

Red Feather squirmed in embarrassment. He knew they were teasing him, joking at his expense.

"Maybe we better take him along next year," suggested Turkey Foot. "Maybe his medicine will help us again."

Finally they grew tired of the joke, and everyone sought his robes. Tomorrow would surely be a turning point, a new beginning on a different portion of the journey. Best of all, they were nearing home.

# 27

>> >> >>

Turkey Foot rode slowly into the river, testing the bottom, while the others watched. Three times he turned his horse away, to try another spot. Finally he seemed certain, and breasted into the current. In a few moments, he was nearly in midstream, and the horse was swimming strongly. Turkey Foot waved in triumph.

Still, they waited. Turkey Foot had been specific in his advice, that they should wait until he was on the opposite shore before trying to cross. So, they noted his point of successful entry and waited. All was going well, the horse swimming strongly. They could plainly see when the horse's flailing hooves struck the river's bottom on the other side. The animal lunged forward, and Turkey Foot leaned over the withers to assist the horse in balancing his weight. They rose out of the river, water streaming from both horse and rider as they moved into shallower depths.

Now they were only a few steps from shore, the current reaching only to the horse's knees. The crossing was all but complete. Then the horse seemed to make a misstep. It stumbled and the front feet sank into some hidden hole. Instantly, the situation was out of control, the horse fighting, and with every movement sinking deeper into the sand.

Turkey Foot half fell, half dived from the horse's back toward the shore, rolling, crawling, swimming in a scramble for solid ground. The horse continued to plunge and struggle. Its hind quarters were sinking. Each time the animal reared to reach with flailing front feet for better footing, its weight pushed its hind feet deeper into the sucking sand. The horse squealed in terror.

Turkey Foot rolled into the shallows and up onto the bank. He sprang to his feet, and the others saw that he had kept his hold on his rope. In anticipation of such an accident, he had placed a rawhide rope around the neck of the horse before entering the stream. Now, as he scrambled to safety, he had maintained his control of the other end.

Skillfully, Turkey Foot tightened the slack from the rope, talking calmly to the horse. Woodchuck began to see the basis of what was needed. The animal must be prevented from rearing up, which would push its hind quarters deeper. It must refrain from the panicky lunging that had become self-defeating. Turkey Foot could assist the horse by constant tension on the rope. This would keep its head down, and in addition, exert a pull in the direction of safety.

The horse struggled again, but this time there was progress in the direction of the bank. It was useful effort, far different from the self-defeating expenditure of a moment ago. Another struggle, and it was apparent that the shore was closer. Turkey Foot took in more slack and retreated to better footing.

In Woodchuck's mind, he could almost see the animal's confidence return. The panic was gone, the dread of the hungry sand that reached to suck its victim under.

At the next effort, it was apparent that the horse's forefeet were striking firmer footing, and it struggled on, pulling its hind feet up and out. In a moment, the animal stumbled out of the water and up on the bank. It stood for a moment, then shook like a wet dog, showering water which sparkled in the sun. There was a shout of victory from Turkey Foot, answered by those on the other shore.

"Wait there," Turkey Foot called.

The warning was needless. No one showed any inclination to start across. He walked along the bank, leaving the horse to graze for a moment. Twice, he took a step or two into the water, and then backed quickly away. Finally, he seemed to be satisfied with the footing.

"Here," he shouted. "Go in where I did, but come out here. One at a time."

There was one exception to the one-at-a-time advice. Woodchuck tied a rope to the neck of Moonflower's horse and handed the end to Red Feather. The girl's inexperience might lead to problems without such a means to assist.

"Now, you follow me," he told his son.

Once the proper places to enter and leave the river were established, there was no problem. They led the pack horses across, and gathered on the north shore with a great deal of relief. It was apparent that the advice of the evening before, to wait until morning, had been sound. Woodchuck shuddered at the thought of attempting such a crossing with night falling. As if to echo his thoughts, Lean Bear spoke.

"*Aiee!* I would not like to do this every day!"

Everyone chuckled. With the danger behind, it was a matter for joking.

"Did you see Turkey Foot rolling in the water?" Bear chided. "He looked like a big fish left stranded in a flood!"

"I did not see you helping!" retorted his cousin. "You can find the crossing next time!"

"No, no," protested Bear. "There is none with your skill in rolling across a stream."

It was mid morning before the excitement had subsided, and all the animals and supplies had been checked. There was, perhaps, a little hesitancy in the parting. Lean Bear finally made the move.

"Well, until next year!" he called, with a final wave.

The two Head Splitters rode away on the westward trail, leading their pack horses. The others watched for a little while, and then mounted to continue their eastward journey. One of the horses nickered a final good-bye to its companions.

The day was good for traveling, the sun warm but not uncomfortable. Moonflower was increasingly surprised at how green the landscape appeared. It was late summer, and in a year with an average amount of rain, the prairie grasses were in their period of growth. Red Feather tried to tell her of grasses in the Sacred Hills which stood taller than a man, but she did not believe him. She was certain that he was teasing.

"No," he insisted. "In the Moon of Ripening, you can ride a horse into the prairie, and the seed heads on the real-grass are taller than the horse. Many times, you can draw a seed stalk of grass from each side and tie them across the horse's back."

"You make a joke of me," Moonflower accused, "because I do not know your grassland."

"No. You will see!" he promised.

In the afternoon, they saw a small band of buffalo a little way to the north.

"Should we try for some meat?" suggested Sky-Eyes.

"Good," Woodchuck agreed. "My mouth is hungry for well-browned hump-ribs."

Red Feather would stay with his wife and the pack horses, it was decided, while the others approached the herd. The two men used different methods. Woodchuck preferred the bow, approaching the running buffalo from the right flank for the kill. Sky-Eyes was more skilled with the lance. His horse, then, was trained to approach from the left of the quarry for the final thrust.

It was a band of cows and calves, and they paused a bowshot away, partly hidden by a low rise, to study the possibilities.

"The fat yearling on the left?" Woodchuck asked.

"Yes, that is good. We both try for that one? If it gets away, we try for any one we can."

"It is good!" Woodchuck muttered as he kneed his horse forward.

The grazing animals raised woolly heads, still chewing, to stare curiously as the riders topped the rise. It was not until they began to retreat that the hunters pushed into a trot, then a gallop in hot pursuit. The selected yearling had managed to lose itself in the middle of the herd, so Sky-Eyes pointed to a young bull, running on the left.

"That one!" he shouted.

He reined in that direction, followed by Woodchuck. In another hundred paces they drew alongside, but Sky-Eyes could not get the proper angle for his thrust. Woodchuck's bow twanged, and the bull stumbled and went down. The rest of the herd rumbled on over the hill and was gone.

"*Aiee!* We eat well tonight!" chortled Woodchuck.

Red Feather and Moonflower rode up with the pack horses.

"Shall we make camp here?" he asked.

"Closer to the river, I think," his father suggested. "We will butcher here and pack some of the meat down to our camp. You and Moonflower can go on down and pick a camp."

The young couple started down the slope.

"Start a fire," Sky-Eyes called after them. "Tonight, we eat well."

"Yes," agreed Woodchuck conversationally, as he began the skinning of their kill. "We are home, Sky-Eyes."

# 28
>> >> >>

Red Feather sat in the starlit prairie and watched the Seven Hunters circle the Real-star. He had taken the first watch, comfortably full from a meal of hump-ribs, their first really pleasurable food for many days. It had been a special thrill for him to introduce such a delicacy to Moonflower.

His wife. He could still hardly believe that he had a wife. So much had happened this summer! There would be much to tell Yellow Head when they reached the Elk-dog band. Some of it he did not really remember, and there were other parts that he remembered in a sort of dream. It had been hard to sort out what had been a dream and what was real. He knew that he had seen his mother. His real mother, not Yellow Head, the step-mother who was the only mother he had ever known. Yes, he had talked to Pink Cloud, and that part was real, without question. Then, was it possible that it was *all* real? For perhaps the hundredth time, he went over it again in his mind, starting with his finding of the flower-shaped medicine object. Then, the blow from the thunder-stick, and his wound.

And, of course, Moonflower. He only dimly remembered how she had hovered over him, pulling him back to the world of the living. Only after that had their friendship ripened into love. He shivered for a moment at that delicious thought. He longed to be with her, thinking of her warm body, now asleep in the sleeping-robes that they shared. No matter. Soon Woodchuck would come to relieve him at the watch, and he would go back to the camp. Moonflower would waken and smile sleepily at him, lifting the edge of the robe to open her arms to him.

He shivered again. He must think of something else, remain alert at the watch. He forced himself to listen to the distant night sounds. Familiar sounds, here in the prairie that was home. There were noises from the north, the yapping of coyotes at the remains of the buffalo kill, the occasional snapping and snarling of disagreement over some choice morsel. Sometimes such a confrontation ended in a yelp of pain as the stronger of the adversaries reinforced rights to the contested delicacy.

All this was good, from the viewpoint of one on watch. As long as the sounds of dissension continued at the kill, it indicated that all was well. Even in the preoccupation of the feeding orgy, nothing would escape the keen senses of the coyote band. So, as long as the feeding sounds continued, it seemed certain that no danger was approaching from the north.

Likewise, the river prevented any unexpected approach from the south. Its quiet murmur was soothing, and a time or two he nearly dozed off, comfortable from a full belly and the relative security of known country. He forced himself to stay awake, listening for other sounds, any sound that might break the lulling sameness of the water's song. A fish jumped, and Red Feather identified its splash. Down river, he heard the hollow cry of *Kookooskoos,* the hunting owl. A bullfrog sounded its mellow boom from the cattails along the shore, and a night bird called somewhere in the thin strip of trees upstream.

He could clearly see the marks of the trail through the grassland, both to the east and west, even in the dim starlight.

Yes, life was good. They had escaped those who pursued them. He wondered some at that entire occurrence.

He did not exactly understand these persistent pursuers who had once been friends of his father's.

And then, there was the odd and dangerous encounter with White Wolf and his warriors. That had been a close call, it seemed, but now this apparently powerful chief was their friend. Such a man could be of great help. It was good that they had managed to establish communication and win his goodwill. Otherwise, coyotes might even now be yapping over the bones of Red Feather and Moonflower and the others, five sleeps south on the Desert Trail. He shivered again, for different reason.

Red Feather saw someone approaching from the direction of the camp. Woodchuck sleepily mumbled a greeting, yawned, and walked a few paces away to empty his bladder. He returned and sat down beside his son.

"Anything happening?"

"No. There are coyotes at the buffalo kill."

"Yes, I hear them."

"The river. That sounds good," Red Feather chuckled.

"Yes," his father agreed. "Sometimes I thought we would never see water again."

"Father," Red Feather spoke seriously, "tell me something of those who hunted after us. I do not quite understand."

Of course, Woodchuck thought. During much of the concern over pursuit by the French, the boy had been unconscious. During his recovery, the others had, perhaps unconsciously, wished to spare him from concern.

"I will tell you," he agreed. "You remember when I came back to the People? You were small, living with your grandparents."

"Yes. You came back, and brought Yellow Head and Sunflower, who became my mother and sister."

"Right. I had been with my own tribe, mine and Sky-Eyes'. I was acting as scout for the leader of an exploring party. Worm-Face, he was called. I left that party, to come home. Pretty Weasel, the man you saw at Santa Fe, became their scout."

"But . . ."

Woodchuck held up a hand in protest.

"Wait. Now, this party at Santa Fe is led by this same Worm-Face."

"Why is he called Worm-Face?"

"Because of hair on his lip."

"Why does he not pluck it?"

"It is their way. It is considered attractive."

"*Aiee!* Yours was a strange tribe, Father! But now, why were they after us?"

"I am not sure. Mostly, I think, because I left them, when I was their scout."

"All those years ago? They still remember?"

"Yes. That is their way. Then, too, your skirmish with them."

"I did not understand that, either. Why did they want to kill me?"

"That was a mistake, I think. Pretty Weasel says they thought you were stealing. Then, you *did* steal their horse."

"I had to."

"Of course. Pretty Weasel returned it."

"Then why did they come after us? I gave back the metal medicine-flower."

Woodchuck pondered a moment.

"I wondered about that, too. My son, I do not know which of us they were after. Maybe both."

"But we have lost them now," Red Feather stated cheerfully.

"Yes. At least, we think so. And now, we are nearly home."

Red Feather rose, yawned, and stretched.

"Well, I must sleep."

"Yes. Sleep well."

He watched the dim shape retreat toward the camp until he lost sight in the starlight.

For a long time he sat listening to the quarreling of the coyotes, the call of the owls in the timber, and the talk of the water. He thought of many things. The talk with his son was especially pleasing to him. He thought it had helped them both to understand the circumstances of their pursuit.

When the first graying of the eastern sky began to indicate that dawn was near, Woodchuck rose and walked around, walking the feeling back into his legs. In the damp of the prairie night, he had stiffened in his sitting position.

The earth began to lighten with the eerie otherworldliness of the false dawn. Distances were deceiving. His gaze swept the surrounding terrain for anything unusual.

He did not see it at first. A rider, approaching from the west, moving slowly. Then he noticed the motion, and began to concentrate on watching the horseman. The horse and rider appeared to be alone. They must have covered a long distance, because the horse fairly staggered with fatigue, and the rider slumped tiredly in the saddle.

In a little while, he must warn the camp, but he would watch a few moments longer. The rider stopped for a moment, and appeared to be listening and looking for something. The coyotes still yapped on the prairie, and this seemed to interest the man. He reined the horse a little aside, and headed almost toward where Woodchuck stood.

At about the same time, Woodchuck recognized something familiar about the horse and the way the rider sat. He waved a greeting.

"Turkey Foot!" he called. "Over here!"

Turkey Foot rode up and the exhausted horse came to a stop. The rider swung down stiffly, and for a moment it seemed that he could not stand.

"What are you doing here?" blurted Woodchuck.

"*Aiee!*" exclaimed the exhausted Turkey Foot. "I am glad I have found you."

"But what . . ."

Turkey Foot held up a hand.

"My friend, Worm-Face and his soldiers are just behind you! One sleep!"

# 29

>> >> >>

"What?" Woodchuck blurted. "On *this* trail?"

"It is true, Woodchuck. We met them on the trail. Your friend, Pretty Weasel, recognized us, we thought, but he said nothing. He asked us of the trail ahead, in sign talk."

"And what did you tell him?"

"Nothing," the other shrugged. "We talked of the weather and the game. Told him we were going home."

"What made you think he knew you, if he said nothing?"

Turkey Foot shrugged again, in his habitual gesture.

"He is a tracker, Woodchuck. A good one, maybe?"

Woodchuck nodded, and the other continued.

"He probably recognized the horses. At the least, he would see that they carried packs, and that the packs did not hold meat or robes or furs."

Woodchuck did not understand.

"But how . . ."

"He would see that we carried trade goods. We were traveling the wrong direction to have trade goods, knives and arrow points. Unless, of course, we just came off the Desert Trail."

"But would he know of that trail?"

"We learned of it. It is no secret, and they were asking in Santa Fe, about trails."

"So you think he knew you, but is still trying to protect us?"

150

Turkey Foot nodded.

"That is what Lean Bear and I believed."

"Did any others know you?"

Turkey Foot shrugged his shoulders again.

"Who knows? I think not. None of them have seen us before. Anyway, we all look alike to them, as Hairfaces do to us."

Woodchuck was amused. Turkey Foot, in dividing people into "we" and "they," had informally placed the two Frenchmen in the "we" group, and the other Frenchmen in "they," along with Spanish and any others who grow fur upon their faces.

"What happened then?"

"Well, after we talked with Weasel, we left them and continued west until we were out of sight. Bear and I decided that we must warn you. He went on with the other animals. I circled back around them and followed you. I heard the coyotes at your kill. Buffalo?"

Woodchuck nodded.

"Yes. Come, we will give you meat."

"Good. I have had no chance to eat."

They walked toward the camp, Turkey Foot leading his tired horse.

"Thank you, my friend," Woodchuck spoke.

"It is nothing." Turkey Foot dismissed his mission with a wave of his hand.

Woodchuck knew better, of course. Turkey Foot had pushed himself to the limit of endurance, and had ridden his horse half to death.

"What are the French doing now?"

"When I last saw them, they were traveling."

"But how could they be here? They took the long way over the pass, while we took the shorter trail."

"They travel fast, Woodchuck. We were moving slowly in the desert. Then we stopped for a day or two. They kept traveling."

They walked in silence until Turkey Foot spoke again.

"I do not understand, Woodchuck. Why do they keep coming after you?"

"I am not sure," Woodchuck mused.

"It cannot be over the stolen horse," Turkey Foot stated. "They have it back. The medicine-flower? It also. I do not know."

He shrugged and walked on.

"Maybe they want me, and not Red Feather," Woodchuck suggested. "You know, I once scouted for them."

"Yes, you had said that. You left them to come home. But anyone should go home if he wants to. Why should they care? And that was long ago."

Yes, thought Woodchuck. Long ago, and in another world. The people of the plains had no understanding of the military obligation he had left when he deserted. Turkey Foot, Lean Bear, Looks Far, none could fathom devotion and duty to a monarch far across the ocean, a loyalty to a chief he had never seen. He had wondered about it himself.

They were nearing the camp, and the others were rising sleepily to start the day.

"Turkey Foot! What are you doing here?" Red Feather asked in astonishment. "Where is Lean Bear?"

Again, Turkey Foot explained the situation, while Moonflower built up the fire and began to place some strips of meat over it.

"So, we must travel," concluded Sky-Eyes. "Turkey Foot, what will you do? Go back, or stay with us?"

"Go home," grunted Turkey Foot, around a mouthful of food. "I have been gone too long. I will rest here a day, maybe. My horse is tired."

"Not too long," suggested Red Feather. "They are coming."

Turkey Foot smiled.

"I will be careful."

He propped more meat near the fire and settled back down to serious eating. Probably, Woodchuck thought, Turkey Foot would spend half the day there, eating and sleeping, and then ride north into the grassland to find a spot where he could continue the same for the rest of the day and night. He might even spend some time confusing their pursuers by placing false signs and tracks at this camp before he left it.

Meanwhile, they must be traveling. Their belongings were quickly packed, and they started east once more.

"Shall we stay on the trail?" Sky-Eyes inquired. "We could try to lose them in the prairie."

"No, it would be no use," Woodchuck reminded. "They have Weasel for a tracker. He would be able to find us."

That, however, was another puzzling thing. Pretty Weasel had saved the life of Red Feather. He appeared to have helped them at the fork of the trail, where the French party continued north. He had again helped by not appearing to recognize Turkey Foot and Bear when they met unexpectedly.

Yet, Weasel was guiding the relentless pursuit. For half the summer, now, his French party had been dogging their trail, day after day, still persistent, with undying determination. Why would Pretty Weasel do this? Sometimes it seemed that there must be two Pretty Weasels. One was loyal, protecting his friend at great risk to himself, gently deluding his employer and misleading the pursuit. On the other hand, there was a Pretty Weasel who had tracked them half the summer, across mountain, desert, and prairie, hunting them down with a bitter determination.

Woodchuck shook his head to clear it. That was crazy thinking. Sometimes he thought he was losing his mind, anyway. The strange feelings he had had when the medicine man was performing his ceremony over the dying Red Feather. It had seemed that one could merely step across into . . . he shook his head again to bring his thought back to reality. Two Pretty Weasels? What nonsense! There must be a logical explanation. Surely. It was only that he could not think of one. Though he tried repeatedly, he could devise not a single theory that would account for all the bizarre happenings of this summer. Or, of course, the strange behavior of his friend Weasel.

At their first meeting, it was true, he and Weasel had tried to kill each other. Could there still be a grudge? No, they had saved each other's lives since. Besides, there had been opportunities for Weasel to wreak vengeance if that was his purpose. Maybe worry was his purpose. There had been nothing since the death of Pink Cloud, when their son was an infant, that had caused so much worry and grief. Until now. But why? And why now?

They stopped only briefly at noon, and moved on, trying to stretch the distance between themselves and their pursuers. They made a good day's travel. Normally, that would have made for a happy evening, a relaxed, good camp. There was water, and grass.

But everyone was tired. The horses were exhausted and recovering slowly because of their poor condition. There was a cloud of gloom over the little camp that evening. One fact was hard to overlook. Although they had made a good day's travel, so had the French. On horses in better condition, traveling well, the relentless pursuers were probably closer than they had been the evening before. Closer, in fact, than at any time since before the Desert Trail.

Yet there was one more devastating discovery before Sun Boy started his next daily run.

Sky-Eyes had relieved Woodchuck at the watch during the night. It was yet a little before dawn, when he heard someone approaching from the camp area. Turning, he quickly identified Red Feather.

"Is my father with you?" asked the youth anxiously. "He is not in his robes."

"Probably went to empty his bladder," suggested Sky-Eyes. "I have not seen him since he left watch."

"No," insisted Red Feather. "I have looked around the camp, and along the river. He is not here."

"But, you know how he likes to go off alone to think." Sky-Eyes tried to sound more confident than he felt. Woodchuck had been behaving strangely.

"No, no, Sky-Eyes. He could do that on watch. Something is wrong."

The situation began to seem even more ominous when daylight also revealed that Woodchuck's horse was missing.

# 30

>> >> >>

When the sun rose, its rays struck directly on the broad shoulders of Woodchuck as he loped westward. He had spent the entire time of his watch in deep thought, and had become more and more troubled.

It was not long after dark when he began to realize that they were involved in a conflict that could not be won. For some time, he had doubted that the persistence of the French pursuit had anything at all to do with Red Feather. No, he decided, from the standpoint of the exploring party, that incident would have been a minor one.

He reconstructed it in his mind, as it would be perceived by one of the voyageurs. A native youth, curious, had approached their camp, and attempted to steal something. He had been caught, with one of the pewter fleur-de-lis baggage seals in his hand. It was unfortunate, the shooting. The marquis was quite upset when he heard of it. The curious thing was that they had never found the boy. He had appeared to be hard hit, but had vanished, practically before their eyes. For a time, it seemed that the wounded boy might have stolen a horse. At least, Luis insisted that his horse was missing. That theory had been dispelled when the scout returned with the horse, which he had found wandering on the trail.

Yes, thought Woodchuck, from the viewpoint of the French, the incident would have gone something like that. He tried a variation or two, but they all led back to the same conclusion. Their pursuers did not know the identity of Red Feather, and probably did not care. This version fit Weasel's description of the shooting, almost an accident.

Next, he thought, if they are not after Red Feather, what is their purpose? This inescapably drew his attention to Weasel again, and the strange way he seemed to be behaving. Assuming, for a moment, that Weasel was not insane, or two different people, what had the scout done to indicate where his loyalties lay? Woodchuck was not quite ready to abandon the more bizarre theories of insanity or double existence. But, if he could explain in a more commonplace fashion, he would be more comfortable.

Going back to their arrival in Santa Fe, Weasel had seen them and contacted them. Then he came to their camp, and it was good to see him. Weasel had attempted to *avoid* a confrontation between Woodchuck and the marquis. When Red Feather was shot, Weasel had protected him, at considerable risk to himself. At the fork of the trail, he appeared to have helped conceal the fact that the traders had taken the Desert Trail.

On the other hand, Weasel had led the pursuit after them. He must have a reason. But *what?* Woodchuck thought about that for a while, trying to think of anything that would affect Weasel, who was largely his own man. In the entire French party, he could think of only one such influence: the marquis himself.

Weasel had been with the marquis for ten years or more, now. And the marquis must be the one urging the pursuit. This led Woodchuck to one more conclusion. There was only one in the trading party actually known to the marquis. Woodchuck. Yes, that must be it! The marquis might actually be unaware of the Red Feather incident. He would, however, be keenly aware of a military deserter.

Now, at last, the pieces began to fit. The marquis, after all these years, had learned that the man he thought dead was, instead, a deserter. And deserters received little quarter. If the marquis returned to France, or even to the outposts in the Great Lakes, able to boast that he had tracked down a renegade . . . that would greatly strengthen the military discipline in all of New France, and even back to Europe. The unremitting pursuit and capture of a deserter after all these years would be quite a story.

Now, he wondered, does this fit with the actions of Pretty Weasel? Yes, he answered himself, of course. Weasel could do nothing to prevent his commander's pursuit, but would try to prevent a confrontation or capture. This would explain every puzzling action on Weasel's part.

After deciding that this must be the explanation, Woodchuck felt better for a while. He would tell Sky-Eyes his theory in the morning. Better yet, when Sky-Eyes came to take his turn at the watch.

With a great deal of satisfaction, Woodchuck relaxed and listened to the night sounds. He was pleased that, at last, he seemed to have solved the riddle which had plagued them since Santa Fe. It was only gradually that he began to realize that this changed nothing. The situation was the same. Less than a day's travel behind them camped the French party of the Marquis de Foixainne. It was a superior force, traveling faster than they. It was many days until they could reach the protection of their own people.

Even then, Woodchuck did not really want an armed clash. He could not, in all conscience, kill his former countrymen, and would not ask his adopted countrymen to do so. He was also unwilling to expose Red Feather and his new bride to such risks.

They could leave the trail, perhaps. But no, they had tried that once. Even the Desert Trail had not deterred the pursuit. The marquis kept coming, coming, as relentlessly as the seasons. Woodchuck felt helpless in the face of such persistence. He felt like a lone buffalo bull he had once watched harried by wolves. The creature was aged and lame, and separated from the herd. It was still strong enough to deter an attack, but the wolves followed relentlessly, giving no rest. Eventually they must pull down the old bull.

And eventually, he now realized, the confrontation with his own past must come. There was no point in prolonging the uncertainty. As he saw more clearly now, he realized that it was his own problem to resolve. He had no right to expose the others to danger, when the marquis wanted only Sergeant Jean Cartier, the deserter, now known as Woodchuck, man of the Elk-dog People. No, the problem was his alone.

By the time Sky-Eyes came to relieve him of watch, he knew what he must do. He went through the motions of small talk with the sleepy Sky-Eyes, and yawned broadly as he turned away in the direction of the camp. Very quietly, he drew near enough to see the sleeping form of his son, cuddled with Moonflower in their warm buffalo robes. He wished that he could talk to them, but it could not be.

"Good-bye, my son," he murmured softly. "May your life be filled with happiness."

He swallowed the lump in his throat, and quietly picked up his saddle. Moonflower stirred, and he froze, waiting until the girl had snuggled closer to her husband, and their breathing had become regular again. Then he moved on, in the direction of the horses.

There was a moment of frustration, as he attempted to catch his horse. The big roan was sometimes temperamental, and Woodchuck considered taking another animal. Finally, though, he was successful in flipping a rope around the gelding's neck, and it quieted. He led it a little farther away from the camp, and saddled quietly. He took the precaution of tying a thong around the muzzle to prevent the animal from nickering. Sky-Eyes would surely notice such a sound, and look for a reason.

Woodchuck led the animal, on foot, for some distance before he stopped to mount. He checked his weapons, and reined the horse to the west, settling into a comfortable lope to gain some distance before they discovered his departure. Then he reined in, to let the horse blow. He would alternate, loping for a while and then walking to rest his mount. This would cover territory efficiently.

He felt that he could estimate the approximate time that he would meet the French party. He had half the night to travel before they would rise and break camp. They were believed to be a short day's travel away. If both he and they traveled at the expected rate of speed, they should meet somewhere near midday.

Then, at last, it would be over. The worrisome cloud that had hung over his head for most of the summer would be lifted. No longer would it endanger his friends and family.

One way or another, it would be over. He checked to verify that his throwing-ax was safely tucked at his waist, and rode on.

# 31
## >> >> >>

"**B**ut where did he go?" Red Feather asked, bewildered. "On a morning hunt?"

Sky-Eyes was thinking rapidly.

"No," he answered quietly. "It is something else."

"But what, Uncle?"

Red Feather used the term as the People used it, a measure of respect when applied to any adult male, especially in a position of authority, regardless of blood kinship. The implication was not lost on Sky-Eyes. Red Feather realized, although perhaps incompletely, that his father was gone. In effect, he was showing his need by recognizing Sky-Eyes as the leader who must answer the questions, make the decisions.

Sky-Eyes wished that it was not so. He did not want this responsibility. First, he must try to explain to the two young people what was happening, when he was not certain himself. Then he must decide what to do. He felt that the trading party was falling apart. Turkey Foot and Lean Bear had gone their own way, as planned. But now even they were separated, each alone to fend for himself. He was not really concerned for them. Both were self-sufficient, and would reach their people in a few sleeps.

The departure of Woodchuck came as a greater blow. He felt that he knew where his friend had gone, but now he must interpret to the others. He was feeling helpless. His instincts told him to follow Woodchuck, to see if he

160

could be of help. Yet, here he was, responsible for the
safety of the two young people. Red Feather was a capable
young man, but inexperienced. He was also still recovering from an almost fatal wound. He was doing well, but
certainly not ready for a fight, if it should come to that.

And Moonflower. The girl was strong and courageous.
Red Feather undoubtedly owed her his life. But, she was
in unknown country. In addition, her status as a woman
was different in her culture. Sky-Eyes was sure that the
women of the pueblos were not taught warrior skills. At
least, not to the extent that they were encouraged in
women of the plains.

Sky-Eyes did not see how he could justify splitting
their tiny force once again. Yet, he felt that he should go
and help Woodchuck. He sighed in frustration. Well, first
things must come first.

"Let us see," he suggested to Red Feather, "if we can
find his tracks."

It took a little time, a frustrating amount of time, but
he felt that it would help Red Feather's acceptance of
their situation. The horses had wandered around the
camp during the night. Their tracks were confused with
the random crisscross of aimless grazing. In addition,
there were few actual areas of open ground where tracks
would be apparent. They circled the camp in widening
arcs, looking for any sign. Finally, well to the west of
camp, they found a man's footprint, next to that of a
horse. Both were pointing west. Another hundred paces
west was another set of tracks.

"He is going west!" Red Feather exclaimed.

"Yes. Listen to me, Red Feather. You know about your
father's old contact with those who follow us?"

"Yes, he told me."

"Good. Now, I think here is what he did. He is not
hunting, or he would have told me before he left. Instead, he led his horse away. This means he wanted a
good start before we missed him. So, it is something he
must do himself."

Red Feather's eyes widened.

"He is going back to fight them, *alone?*"

"Maybe not fight them. Maybe only talk to them."

"But, we cannot let him do this."

"He gave us no choice."

"We must go back to help him!"

"I must, Red Feather. You take your wife and go ahead. You know where to find the People. We will follow, later."

He knew that the last part of the statement was probably untrue. He did not see how they could extricate themselves from this situation, but he had to try. Even, he admitted regretfully, if it came to a fight.

"No!" Red Feather declared with finality. "We will go with you."

Sky-Eyes smiled inwardly. The boy was much like his father, in his stubborn determination. Once Woodchuck had set his mind, there was no use trying to change it. Well, it should be Red Feather's choice, he decided. It was his father they were trying to help.

"It is good," he stated, past the lump in his throat. "Let us ride."

A day's journey to the west, the marquis and his party were also rising to greet the sun.

Pretty Weasel was troubled. It seemed to him that he had spent the entire summer trying to keep his friends from killing each other. In Santa Fe, it had pleased him greatly that he had managed to prevent a meeting of Woodchuck and Worm-Face.

Then, by the worst of evil happenings, the boy Red Feather, son of his friend, had blundered into the French camp. That had been a risky thing. He had expected the boy to die, but someone's medicine had been strong.

Weasel had tried to delay their departure from Santa Fe as long as he could. So long, in fact, that the marquis had become irritable over it, and had suggested that he was malingering. When they finally moved on, past Blue Corn's pueblo, Weasel was alarmed to find the party of Woodchuck only a day ahead of them.

He could delay travel no longer. The time would come, he knew, when the party ahead of them would experience a slow day. A lame horse, a stop to hunt for supplies, any slight delay, and the French party would overtake them.

He was still worrying about that when they came to the place where there were no more tracks in the trail ahead of them. It took him half a day to unravel that mystery, and find the Desert Trail. Weasel chuckled to himself. One or more of the men in Woodchuck's party were skilled trackers. He was greatly pleased. He had heard of this other trail, in Santa Fe, but it had sounded risky. He had advised against it.

Now, that was good. Those ahead must know they were followed, and had wisely chosen this as an escape. It was good. He could relax now in the knowledge that his friend Woodchuck was on another trail, out of harm's way.

There had been one other confrontation between Weasel and the marquis. When they reached the *Ar-kenzes* River, Weasel had suggested that they continue north, through known country, and retrace their previous route down the Platte. Worm-Face was adamant. They must follow the trail they were now traveling, down the *Ar-kenzes*, to explore new territory. Worm-Face was drawing lines in a book of talking leaves to show where they had been.

Weasel's concern was that Woodchuck had told him of this trail. It was said to run through the country of the People. Well, no matter, he finally decided. It is a big country. The chances of encounter would be very slim. They turned east, following the trail along the *Ar-kenzes*.

He was astonished to encounter, one otherwise ordinary day, the two Head Splitters from Woodchuck's party. They were traveling *west*, which puzzled him for a little while. He dared not carry on too explicit a conversation with them, because some of the voyageurs had learned a little sign talk. When they parted, he had gathered only that the rest of the party was alive. If these men were traveling west, the others must be going east, and were ahead of them on the trail again.

That had been two sleeps ago, and he was still troubled. He thought of riding ahead to warn them, but could think of no way to explain his absence. He would be gone a day and a night.

They stopped for a noon rest, and Weasel lay in the shade of an old, giant cottonwood and tried to think of a plan. His eyes were closed, but his senses acute. He heard the hoofbeats at almost the same time one of the voyageurs spoke.

"Look! Someone comes."

Weasel sat up, and then sprang to his feet in alarm. The rider was Woodchuck.

The horseman rode into their noon camp without a word, straight toward the seated marquis. A couple of the voyageurs moved in that direction, hands ready at their weapons, but the newcomer showed no overt signs of hostility.

Pretty Weasel hurried to the spot. He did not know what he might do, or what would happen next. He had a panicky feeling, however, that whatever was about to happen would not be good.

# 32
>> >> >>

**W**oodchuck rode into the French noon camp with his heart pounding and palms sweating. He felt that his entire life for the past fifteen years had centered on this moment. He noted the curious stares of the voyageurs, curious but not unduly alarmed. There was little danger from a single horseman, riding calmly into camp without show of violence.

He could imagine their thoughts: a native, in buckskins, well mounted, armed, and his hair plaited in the manner of one of the buffalo-hunter tribes. They might be confused by his blue-gray eyes, but would probably assume him to be a half-breed. Well, it was no matter, now.

Pretty Weasel scrambled to his feet and moved to intercept Woodchuck's advance toward the marquis if it became necessary. A couple of the voyageurs did the same. Not aggressively, just cautiously. They were doing their jobs well. To forestall any violence, Woodchuck raised his hand in the sign for peaceful greeting. He rode directly to the place where the marquis was seated.

"Monsieur," he stated, "your chase is over."

A look of utter astonishment came over the face of the marquis. Probably the last thing on earth that he expected during the noon halt was a native, riding in out of the prairie, and addressing him in flawless French.

"*Sacrebleu!*" he exclaimed. "What is this?"

"I have been running too long," continued Wood-chuck. "It is over."

He paused to take a deep breath.

"I was right to rejoin my family," he went on, "and I am prepared to fight for that right. I will meet anyone here in combat." He made a sweeping gesture to include the entire company. "Even you, monsieur. But, I will not be taken without a fight."

The look of astonishment had never left the face of the marquis, but to some extent he now regained his composure. When he spoke, it was with the dignity of his position.

"Your courage is admirable, monsieur," he said smoothly, "but why would you want to fight me? Who in God's name *are* you anyway?"

Woodchuck straightened in the saddle.

"Sergeant Jean Cartier, monsieur. You know me well."

*"Mon Dieu,* Sergeant," the marquis exploded, "I never saw you before in my life!"

Sudden, bitter understanding flooded through Wood-chuck's thoughts. He had made a mistake, a tragic misin-terpretation of events. He had not been pursued at all, was not sought as a deserter. That incident, now so long ago, had been completely forgotten. It was so minor that the marquis did not even remember it. Apparently there was no pursuit, and never had been. The two parties had merely been traveling the same direction, with only Pretty Weasel aware of the identity of those ahead. And Pretty Weasel, of course, could say nothing, because he, too, had misinterpreted . . . *aiee,* what a disaster this had become!

Where no problem had been, Woodchuck had blun-dered in, proclaiming himself a deserter. Now, there was a major crisis of his own making. Not only had the mar-quis forgotten the incident, but no one knew his name. Until, of course, he had blatantly announced his name and rank to the whole company. Now, there was no way out. How, he asked himself desperately, could he have been so stupid? He had an impulse to turn and run, but knew that it would not do. So he sat, feeling more and more foolish. The puzzled marquis looked from Woodchuck to Pretty Weasel and back again. Weasel stood, still alarmed, wondering what would happen next.

Then a light of understanding began to dawn on the face of the marquis.

"Wait," he muttered, half to himself. "Yes . . . I remember now. Woodchuck! The river! You taught me sign talk! Told me my name . . . Worm-Face!" He paused to roar with laughter. "My God, Sergeant, what happened? Where have you been? We thought you were dead!"

Woodchuck sat staring in disbelief. He looked to Pretty Weasel, who looked equally puzzled, and back to the jubilant marquis.

"Get down, Sergeant! Join us! Tell me about yourself!"

Cautiously, Woodchuck dismounted. All his mistrust and suspicion could not be dispelled instantly. He handed his horse's rein to Weasel, and sat with the marquis where the latter indicated.

"Now tell me," urged the marquis, "you rejoined your family?"

"My family? Yes," mumbled the confused Woodchuck.

"You once mentioned a son, I believe. You found him?"

"Yes. He is grown now. He has a wife."

"Ah, young love!" exclaimed the marquis. "But, we thought you were dead. You had only gone to find your family, no?"

He stopped to laugh again, and then continued his questions.

"But how . . . ah, yes . . . Weasel knew!"

He looked over at the uncomfortable scout.

"You helped him! Scoundrels!"

He roared with laughter, and then became serious.

"Look, we must talk. You can be of great help to me."

"Monsieur, I will not . . ."

"No, no, I will not ask you to go back. You are still living with your wife's people?"

"Yes, sir. My first wife had been killed before. I have remarried."

"Good. And you know the plains?"

"Yes, some. We travel them."

Where was this leading?

"You know that I am exploring. I just came from Santa Fe. Spanish colony."

"Yes, sir. We trade there. Knives, steel tools."

The eyes of the marquis widened in surprise.

"Good! My purpose is twofold. First to map, then to consider the possibility of trade with Spain. You have anticipated both."

"Not really, monsieur. But where? Where are the French posts who would trade?"

"There are none. But if it seems practical, we would colonize. On the rivers. The *Missi-sepe,* the "Great River," possibly the *Miss-ouree.* We were treated well by the Spanish. Do you think this possible?"

Be cautious, now, Woodchuck told himself. The possibility of trade would be a mixed blessing. The possession of metal tools was highly desirable, but the influence on the People and their way of life was a nagging worry to him. Once before, he had faced this dilemma. Red Feather was only an infant when Sergeant Cartier started back with the military report on their exploration of the prairie. He had burned the journal and falsified his oral report, to protect his dead wife's people.

Things were different now. Both France and Spain were exploring the plains. The People must have contact with civilization. He and Sky-Eyes had fostered it themselves, with their first trading venture. Since it would happen anyway, would it not be good to be active participants, to retain some semblance of control?

"I think it is possible," he told the marquis.

"Excellent! Let us camp here," he called to the voyageurs. "Weasel, see if you can find a buffalo. We will stay here to talk of this. Maybe a day or two, no?"

He turned back to Woodchuck.

"Which way are you traveling? Are your people near here?"

It was disconcerting, the way the marquis could become excited, asking more questions before his previous ones could be answered. At the moment, Woodchuck could scarcely remember what he *had* been doing.

"We were traveling east, monsieur."

"But you were going west when you rode in just now."

"Yes, well, I retraced our steps because . . ."

"Never mind."

The marquis was off on another train of thought.

"Where are your people?"

"They are in summer camp, a place called Walnut River."

He paused to describe the location and distance.

They were still discussing the topography of the area, poring over the sketch maps of the marquis, when one of the voyageurs came loping in.

"We have a buffalo kill, monsieur. They are butchering now. But I came to tell you, there are people coming."

"People?"

"Yes. Three riders, with two pack horses. From the east."

Woodchuck was certain he knew this party. He was just beginning to try an explanation when a lone rider appeared, loping toward the camp. He recognized the way the man sat on his horse, the erect posture that was the result of military discipline.

"Sky-Eyes!" murmured Woodchuck to himself.

He turned to the marquis.

"Monsieur, I must tell you . . ."

The marquis waved him aside. The rider came to a sliding stop before them.

"Monsieur," began the newcomer in polished French, "I am Lieutenant André Du Pres. I would speak in behalf of this man. I must share in any guilt of his, as he was under my command."

"My God," moaned the marquis. *"Another* one?"

The homecoming was a great celebration that year, when the traders returned from Santa Fe. The wolves had observed the travelers a day before they reached the summer camp of the Elk-dog band. At first there was confusion, because the party of travelers was large. Soon, however, the scouts had determined that this was, indeed, Sky-Eyes, Woodchuck, and Red Feather, with two pack horses.

They rode with a party of warriors, men of an unknown tribe, and it was seen that some had hair upon their faces. Since they seemed congenial, it was assumed that they were traveling together under friendly circumstances.

There was one other puzzling thing. Red Dog and Broken Lance discussed it from their vantage point behind the crest of the ridge. It concerned a youth who rode beside Red Feather.

"He rides one of their pack horses," observed Broken Lance. "Remember, the one with the star on its face and three white feet?"

"Yes, you are right. He seems an inexperienced rider."

"Somebody they picked up."

"I suppose."

It was noon before the scouts showed themselves and approached the column of travelers. Greetings were jovial.

"*Ah-koh*, Sky-Eyes, Woodchuck, how goes it?"

"It is good, Red Dog. We have much to tell."

It was only then that they saw that the other rider was a woman.

"Red Feather's wife," explained Woodchuck. "Her name is Moonflower."

"*Aiee*, you do have much to tell! Who are these others?"

"Men of our tribe. Mine and Sky-Eyes'. This is their leader, Chief Worm-Face."

Broken Lance and Red Dog gave the sign of greeting, which the marquis returned.

"It is too bad," Broken Lance observed. "He is otherwise not bad-looking."

"What?"

"His face. An old injury?"

"No," Sky-Eyes smiled. "That is their way. They think it makes him handsome. They shape the face-hair instead of plucking it."

"*Aiee!* How strange!"

Broken Lance was studying the moustache.

"How does he form the sharp points on the ends?"

"What is it?" asked the marquis in French, puzzled at the attention.

"He is admiring your moustache, monsieur. He wishes to know how you shape the points," explained Sky-Eyes.

The marquis roared with laughter.

"I wax it! Will he understand?"

"Yes, I think so."

He turned and explained the use of moustache wax.

"How strange!" Broken Lance observed. "But not entirely bad."

Sky-Eyes had the strong feeling that Broken Lance was tempted to try a waxed moustache himself if opportunity offered.

Red Dog set off to carry the news of the trading party's return. Consequently, when they neared the village that evening, they were met by a welcoming party. A dozen young warriors on their best horses, in paint and finery, charged toward the approaching column, yelling the deep-throated war cry of the People.

"It is a welcoming ceremony!" Sky-Eyes called in French. "Just ride on!"

He and Woodchuck rode back along the column, reassuring the nervous voyageurs, as the warriors circled and whooped.

People on foot began to straggle out to meet them, accompanied by running children and barking dogs. The welcoming warriors finally stopped circling and formed a loosely knit escort on each side of the French party.

Word had quickly spread that the visitors were from the tribe of Sky-Eyes and Woodchuck. A welcoming celebration was in the making. Meat was cooking already, and there would be speeches and dancing until far into the night.

No one, of course, was happier to see the returning men than their families. Pale Star and Yellow Head hurried out to meet their men. Yellow Head shed a few tears over the loss of her stepson to another woman, but at the same time welcomed Moonflower to her lodge with open arms. The young couple would live there until their own lodge could be established.

There were introductions of the marquis and the voyageurs, who were to be treated as honored guests. They were welcomed by White Hawk as chief of the Elk-dog band, and by the aging Looks Far, whose medicine had guided and advised three generations. He predicted good medicine between the two peoples.

Pale Star was a bit dubious. She and Sky-Eyes talked at great length that night, cuddled in each other's arms while they listened to the songs and the rhythmic beat of the dance drum.

"Is this wise, Sky-Eyes, to bring the French? I know they are your people, but it brings many problems."

Sky-Eyes was quiet a long time.

"Star," he began finally, "we have no choice. We need the trade they will bring. Someone will come, sometime, and it may as well be someone we know and trust."

This was a big step for both Sky-Eyes and Woodchuck.

They had talked of it on the way home. Both, as well as Pale Star, feared and resented the intrusion of civilization into the world of the People. Still, it must be accepted, for the good things it would bring. Already, steel knives and axes were in common use, gained by laborious trips to trade with the Spanish. It would be much easier to trade with the French near their own territory.

Sky-Eyes understood his wife's problem. She had lived among the French for several years, first as a virtual slave of the crazed Three Owls, then as the wife of Brûle, the scout. Her entire life for those years had been devoted to a plan to leave the French and *Mishi-ghan*, and return to the broad prairies and open skies of the grassland. Seeing the French today must have brought back many unwanted memories. He cradled her tenderly in his arms.

"Well, what will be will be," Star said with a sigh. "Nothing stays the same. But I had hoped that our children might live in a time less confusing than ours."

"Does that time ever come?" he asked.

"No. But, there is something . . . I do not know, Sky-Eyes."

"You have a vision-feeling for this?"

Pale Star was considered by her uncle, the medicine man, to have special senses for seeing the future. She had not welcomed this psychic ability, but Sky-Eyes had grown to understand that when it appeared, it was important to listen to his wife's premonitions.

"I do not know," she said slowly. "I feel danger. Tragedy. But not to us, somehow."

"To whom, then? Woodchuck's family?"

"No. They have had theirs. *Aiee,* that was worrisome to me. I did not know . . . but, never mind. Come, let us make love."

It was not until past the Moon of Falling Leaves, well into the Moon of Madness, that they came to an understanding of Pale Star's premonition. A traveler whom they encountered on the way south to winter camp told the story.

The French party had met with tragedy. On the jour-

ney back up the Great River, the *Missi-sepe,* there had
been an accident. One of their warriors had dropped a
thunder-stick as he stepped out of a canoe, and the
weapon had accidently discharged its medicine. Their
chief, who was called Worm-Face, was struck by the pro-
jectile, and died next day.

The news struck Woodchuck harder than anyone. He
could hardly imagine the bombastic marquis struck
down, his boundless energy stilled by death.

"What did the others do?" he asked.

"They buried him, by the river," the traveler related.
"I suppose they went home."

Woodchuck's heart was heavy for the man he would
have unhesitatingly killed only a few moons before if
occasion had demanded. He had come to understand the
marquis. In his own way, Worm-Face understood the
frontier and the prairie beyond. He would never have
become a part of it, as Woodchuck and Sky-Eyes had
done, but he understood it as few Europeans had come to
do. Now he would rest beside the Great River he had
loved, in the middle of a continent far from home that
had become the most important force in his life.

The People mourned the passing of Worm-Face, the
strange yet exciting foreigner who had been with them
for a short while. They sang the traditional Song of
Mourning in his honor. At the next naming ceremony,
an old man did not bestow his own name on his grandson, as was expected. The child was titled Worm-Face, in
honor of the departed chief, and it was good.

At the next Sun Dance, Woodchuck sacrificed a carved
medicine stick to the memory of the man he had come to
respect and love. There were those who said that the
carving on this stick was Woodchuck's finest work.

Perhaps, though, the greatest impact of Worm-Face's
death was in the area of events that did not happen.
Without his dynamic urge to push to the west, there was
none to do so. It would be yet another generation before
the fleur-de-lis would find its way again to the banks of
the *Miss-ouree.*

# GENEALOGY

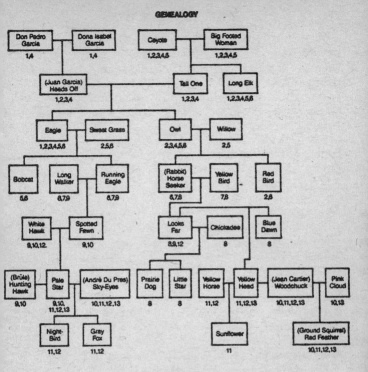

## Dates for Volumes in the Spanish Bit Saga

Dates are only approximate, since the People have no written calendar.
Characters in the Genealogy appear in the volumes indicated.

A proud people in a proud land

# THE SPANISH BIT SAGA

Set in the New World of the sixteenth and seventeenth centuries, Don Coldsmith's acclaimed novels recreate a time, a place, and a people that have been nearly lost to history. In *The Spanish Bit Saga* we see history through the eyes of the proud Native Americans who lived it.

Turn the page for an exciting preview of *Trail From Taos*, Book 14 in Don Coldsmith's *The Spanish Bit Saga*, to be published in December 1990. It will be available wherever Bantam Books are sold.

*Number 14 of the Spanish Bit Saga*
*Time period: 1680, about twenty years after*
The Flower in the Mountains

# 1

>> >> >>

**R**ed Feather led his caravan over the crest of the ridge and paused to let the horses blow after the steep ascent. It was a good place to stop and rest, and to become accustomed to the spectacular scene that stretched below. It was familiar, after the almost yearly expedition to Santa Fe to trade, yet always different. And, of course, so very different from the lush tallgrass prairie of home.

It seemed only a short while ago that he had stood at his father's side on this ridge and first experienced the sight of the plain below. He smiled to himself at the memory of that trip. He had been so young, so naïve. His inexperience had nearly gotten him killed. He looked back over his shoulder and waved to his wife. Moonflower smiled and waved back, then kneed her horse forward to join him. It had been her stubborn refusal to let him die that had saved him.

Now, many winters later, their own children were nearly grown. Moonflower had decided to accompany the pack train, to visit her people at the pueblo while the others went on into Santa Fe to trade.

It was a good season, he thought with satisfaction. The pack train, laden with furs and tanned robes, numbered sixteen pack animals, not counting those they were riding. This was the largest trading venture ever attempted by the People, he believed, and he was proud to lead it. The young men learned well.

He watched Swallow and Yellow Robe move from one

horse to another, checking packs and cinches. Their allies, the Head Splitters from the shortgrass country to the west of the People, had always joined in the annual expedition. There was old Turkey Foot, who had been on the very first expedition. The younger Head Splitters, Red Dog and Bull's Horn, were also rapidly becoming skilled at packing and handling the horses.

Moonflower now reined in beside him, her face shining with excitement.

"You look happy," he observed, teasing her. "What is the matter, woman, you are not tired from the journey?"

Moonflower smiled, the smile he loved to see, which crinkled the little lines at the corners of her eyes.

"Of course I am happy," she chided. "I am going home."

"You are leaving me?" he asked in mock alarm.

She laughed, showing even white teeth. She was still beautiful, Red Feather thought, even though they were both well past thirty winters.

"You cannot get rid of me so easily," she warned.

It was an exchange of long standing between them. He knew that it had been difficult for her, living far away from her home and her family, among customs unfamiliar to her. He had tried to let her know by this good-natured bantering that he understood. It had become a game between them, an open statement of respect for each other's feelings. It had helped to make theirs a happy lodge.

"My parents grow older," Moonflower said more seriously.

Red Feather nodded. Moonflower had not seen her people for several seasons. Blue Corn, his wife's father, had seemed old when first they met. He was a chief, the leader of the small pueblo a day's ride from the town of Santa Fe. Chiefs of Moonflower's people, Red Feather knew, held somewhat different status from chiefs of the buffalo hunters of the prairie. There was much that he did not understand about it. Sometimes it seemed to him that Blue Corn's position as leader of his cluster of earthen lodges held very little actual meaning. The major decisions were guided principally by the medicine men.

Yet somehow, Blue Corn did hold a place of respect that was unique in his village. His was a calm, quiet dignity, an inner strength. He asked for no trouble, and gave none. Blue Corn's people had survived for many generations in this location beside the great Southwest Trail, by tolerance of all who passed. He was known to the Spanish military patrols who made this village the northernmost point of their circuit. The soldiers were tolerant of Blue Corn's village and its people, because no trouble had ever occurred there.

At the same time, he had maintained good relations with the militant reactionaries over the mountain at the Taos pueblo. There was a nucleus of fiery anti-Spanish sentiment there which had seemed to be growing the past few seasons.

When the People first came to trade, a generation ago, Blue Corn had befriended the strangers from the prairie, given them directions, traded supplies. He possessed great wisdom, but seldom shared it unless it was asked. To Red Feather, the man had always seemed a solid dependable rock in the midst of a strange and unfamiliar landscape. No, not like a rock. Like a great tree, perhaps. But that did not quite fit, either.

Red Feather had been walking with Blue Corn one morning after a storm, a few seasons ago. The travelers had seen the approach of Rain Maker, and heard the rumble of his drum across the distant mountains. They had hurried to reach the shelter of Blue Corn's pueblo before the storm struck. The next morning, the two men had walked beside the rushing stream that was usually a dry and sandy bed. They came to a giant cottonwood which had been split and shattered by the force of the wind, and lay broken, half of it prostrate on the ground. Red Feather had remarked that the willows along the creek had fared better.

"Ah, yes," Blue Corn observed. "The willows bend as far as they must, while the cottonwood stands firm."

"I do not understand, Uncle."

"Look!" the older man advised. "By bending, they do not break. The willows will be here after the mighty cottonwood is broken."

"It is better, then," Red Feather answered, "that they bend to avoid breaking?"

Blue Corn shrugged, a twinkle in his eye.

"If you are a willow," he observed mischievously.

That, Red Feather finally decided, was the secret of Blue Corn's success. He was flexible. Like the willow, he would bend to avoid being broken, and would thus succeed. In this way he had maintained the respect and good will of the Spanish, the militant faction of his own people, and the traders from the plains. Through the years Red Feather had an increasing respect for the wisdom of this remarkable man.

"Let us move on," Red Feather announced after they had rested for a little while.

The pack train stirred into motion and began to file down the south slope of the ridge. The trail was plain, and the pack horses so well accustomed to the routine by this time that they made no effort at all to stray.

It was still several sleeps before they neared the village that had been Moonflower's home. She became more and more excited, and finally one morning, could stand it no longer.

"Could we ride ahead, my husband? I long to see my father and mother."

Red Feather smiled. There was no reason to object. The trail was plain, and there were no enemies in the entire area.

"Of course!" he agreed. "Turkey Foot can lead the pack train."

He loped back to confer with Turkey Foot, and quickly returned.

"It is good!" he reported with a smile. "Let us go!"

They cantered ahead. Moonflower, who had been completely unfamiliar with horses at the time they married, had learned rapidly. She now enjoyed the freedom of travel that the plains customs of her husband's tribe demanded. Their entire lives were centered around the buffalo and the horse. So it happened that they moved rapidly ahead of the pack train and reached the pueblo nearly half a day in advance.

Moonflower's parents came from the doorway to greet them as they approached. She kneed the horse forward, jumping down to run and embrace her mother.

"Where are the children?" the older woman asked. "Are they not with you?"

"Only White Fox," Moonflower explained. "He is a half-day behind us, with the pack train. Elk Woman has her own lodge."

"He is old enough to do this?" the boy's grandmother marveled.

"He thinks so," Moonflower laughed. "He felt that he was needed to help while we came on ahead."

Red Feather was exchanging greetings with his father-in-law.

"You have had a good journey?" Blue Corn inquired.

"Yes, Uncle. We have traveled well. And our furs are prime. Our best packs yet."

He paused, noting a lack of enthusiasm on the part of the other man. Something must be wrong.

"Uncle," he ventured, "what is it? Is it not well with you?"

Blue Corn heaved a deep sigh of resignation. He nodded gently.

"With us, yes. It is not that, my son. But these are troubled times."

"Trouble?" Red Feather blurted.

"Yes. You know it has been coming. Blood has been shed. It may not be possible for you to trade in Santa Fe."

**2**

>> >> >>

"**Y**es, these are troubled times," Blue Corn was saying.

The travelers had rested and eaten, and now the two men walked along the stream to talk. Red Feather had come to look forward to these visits, short and infrequent though they might be. There was something of stability in the way Blue Corn walked the sandy path that he had walked since childhood. Something of immortality, it seemed. It had taken much understanding on the part of the young Red Feather. It was almost beyond his comprehension that these lodges of earthen bricks had stood in one spot for many generations. The lodges of the People were moved with the seasons, migrating with the buffalo and then choosing a desirable area in which to winter. Here, there was inescapable sameness.

They passed the rotting stump of the giant cottonwood which had been the subject of a conversation long ago. Red Feather saw, a few paces away, a sapling as tall as his head. Its leaves quivered in the breeze, and he wondered idly how long it would be until this sturdy newcomer would become a tree which could replace the shady canopy of the dead giant. More generations. How many generations of Blue Corn's people had seen these trees grow to maturity, shade their children, fall into the silver-gray of death and decay, and then be replaced?

In a way, he realized, it was much like the yearly cycle of the grass. The long nights of winter were followed by the Moon of Awakening, and the greening of the new grass. Then the buffalo would return to eat, grow fat, and be harvested by the People and their four-legged brothers. The Moon of Falling Leaves would signal the last phase, with the grasses going dormant and the buffalo disappearing for the winter. The People would enter winter camp, to wait for the cycle to repeat next season.

Of course, Blue Corn's people of the pueblo lived by a yearly cycle of growing crops, too. But Red Feather was just beginning to understand the timelessness of their way of life. The pueblo's lodges had been there for many winters, their spirit renewed by each generation in turn. Just as the children of each generation had been shaded at play by new generations of cottonwoods.

"What will you do now?" Blue Corn asked.

Red Feather looked up in surprise.

"Go to Santa Fe," he stated flatly. "We have come to trade!"

Blue Corn, never one to argue, nodded tentatively, then spoke again.

"It may be dangerous."

"I think not, Uncle. Look, we have always been friends of the Spanish, since my father and Sky-Eyes began the trading."

Blue Corn nodded again.

"But," he pointed out, "those who hate the Spanish may object to your trading with them."

"Your people?"

"Yes. My people have been badly treated, many generations. You remember Popé, the Elder from the Tewas?"

Red Feather nodded.

"He saved my life when I was wounded."

"He is back in Taos. You knew he had been in prison in Santa Fe?"

"But was he not released last year?"

Blue Corn nodded.

"Yes, but he is bitter. When he was caged, you know, several others were beaten. Three Elders were killed with the rope."

Blue Corn's eyes reflected the horror of such a death by hanging. Their spirits would be unable to escape the body, he explained, because of the constriction of the rope around the neck.

"Aiee!" Red Feather murmured. "What is Popé doing in Taos?"

"He is stirring up the young men to resist the Spanish," Blue Corn explained. "It is a thing of the spirit."

"I do not understand, Uncle."

"The Spanish elders, you know, the ones who wear this sign"—he paused to trace a cross in the sand with his finger—"they tell the young that our ways are bad."

"But why, Uncle? Why would they do that?"

Blue Corn shrugged.

"I do not know. I have noticed this myself. They want to tell their story, but will listen to no one else's."

"Theirs is a good story," observed Red Feather. "That of First Man and First Woman, and the real-snake. Also, that part about the chief who rises from the dead."

"A good story," Blue Corn agreed. "But why, then, do they not wish to listen to ours, or yours?"

Both shook their heads in nonunderstanding. It would be only polite to exchange creation legends around the story fires. This was an expected form of entertainment among both the People and those of the pueblos. To encounter a tribe who refused to listen . . . *aiee!*

"Well," Blue Corn continued, "Popé, you remember, has always been worried that the Spanish want our young people to give up the old ways. The prayers, the ceremonies, the spirit-talk. Popé says we will lose the spirit-ways that are ours, and the young will forget. So he talks and stirs up the young men."

He walked a little way in silence, head down, dejected.

"For many seasons, Popé only counseled against listening to the Spanish medicine men," he continued. "Now, he urges violence."

"But, Uncle, that would only be against the Spanish. Your people and mine are friends."

Blue Corn nodded.

"Yes, but . . . I do not know, Red Feather. They may oppose your trading with the Spanish."

"How could that harm them?"

Blue Corn shrugged.

"In things of the spirit, men do not think clearly."

"But we must trade," Red Feather insisted. "Uncle, this is our biggest train. Sixteen pack horses, heavy packs of prime furs and robes, ours and the Head Splitters'. There is nothing else to do with them. And we need the metal tools."

Blue Corn was silent a little longer, but finally answered.

"You do what you must. But, my son, I fear these times are evil. It is past the fork in the path where our people can say, 'no, we do not want your medicine.' Blood has been shed."

"Yes, tell me of that."

"I do not know. We hear things. Since the Spanish killed our Elders, there is much hate. The Spanish patrols do not come out this far anymore. They are afraid. An arrow from the darkness . . . then they catch and kill one of our people. The wrong one, of course, and this calls for vengeance. It is bad."

Red Feather had not realized that the situation had deteriorated this far.

"But still, Uncle, we are friends of both sides. Surely, this is not our fight, and we are in no danger. We deal with the trader and with the soldiers, not the medicine men. We will go to Santa Fe, do our trading, and leave quickly."

"Do what you must," Blue Corn said again, unconvinced. "But remember, my son, when dogs fight, anyone interfering may be bitten."

"I do not wish to interfere, Uncle. This is their argument, not ours."

Blue Corn did not answer. He had stated his position, and obviously saw no need to continue the conversation.

Another thought struck Red Feather.

"Uncle, how is it that your pueblo has escaped this?"

Blue Corn sighed.

"We have tried to do as they wish. Their priests come and tell their stories, and we listen. We do our sacred songs and dances only in secret. But now, this enrages those who follow Popé. He wants us to resist, to refuse to listen to the Spanish medicine men. But if we do, then the Spanish soldiers beat or kill us."

Red Feather slowly began to understand the precarious position of Blue Corn's village.

"Uncle," he said quietly, "you are right. These are evil times."

# 3

>> >> >>

One moment the sandy slope was empty, with no living thing in sight, except a distant eagle drawing his circles in the blue of the mountain sky. The next, it was populated by heavily armed men. There were at least twenty of them, carrying bows, a few with spears, and all wearing knives at their waists. They had seemed to sprout magically from behind the red-brown rocks, from the silvery greasewood which straggled along the slope, and even from the soil itself.

Red Feather tried to appear calm as he reined in his horse. This encounter was a total surprise, though it should have been expected, he told himself irritably. He looked back along the wavering line of pack animals. The other men were reacting calmly, as he would expect. Long generations of confrontation on the prairie had established custom in such a meeting. They would wait while the leaders met and talked, and then act according to how that conversation developed.

A tall young man, flanked by two companions, now strode confidently down the slope toward Red Feather's horse. The others waited, weapons ready. Red Feather was irritated, partly at himself. He should have had outriders scouting ahead and to the sides. The People called them "wolves," these scouts who circled the main column like wolves circling a moving herd of buffalo. Yes, he should have had wolves out.

The young leader of the strangers was dressed in the loose tunic and leggings of the pueblo people. Good, thought Red Feather. At least, I know their customs.

"Who are you? Where are you going?" barked the young man in Spanish.

Red Feather's anger flared, and he made a concerted effort to calm himself before he answered. This abrupt demand was quite impolite and demeaning. In addition, there was an implied insult in the man's choice of Spanish to address strangers. These were, in all likelihood, some of the revolutionaries led by Popé. That he would address strangers in Spanish implied that they were already considered enemies. Red Feather recalled that Popé himself was said to refuse the use of the Spanish tongue, though he understood it fluently.

Red Feather drew himself up tall in the saddle and tried to appear as dignified as possible.

"I am Red Feather, of a tribe far to the east," he said calmly.

He used the language of his wife's pueblo people. This would, hopefully at least, strengthen the idea that they were friends, if not allies. The other man seemed startled for a moment, then quickly recovered his composure.

"How is it that you speak our tongue?" he asked, in a slightly less abrasive tone.

"It is my wife's language," Red Feather replied stiffly. "Her father's name is Blue Corn."

"Ah, yes," nodded the young man. "I know of him. A good man, it is said, though he deals with the Spanish."

A look of realization crossed the dark face, and he glanced at the pack horses.

"What is in your packs?" he demanded suspiciously. "Supplies for the Spanish?"

"Of course not!" Red Feather snapped. "We have furs and robes, to trade for the things we need. Metal knives, arrow points, spearheads."

For the first time, a broad smile lit the face of the other man.

"Weapons!" he chortled. "Good! We can use more weapons."

Red Feather, seething inwardly, held his temper in check. This was no time to cause an argument by pointing out that the packs, and whatever merchandise might result from their trade, were the property of the People and their allies, the Head Splitters. Certainly, he had no intention of turning the proceeds over to some roving band of fanatics. But it seemed prudent to keep such thoughts quiet for the present. He was thinking rapidly ahead. After they finished trading, perhaps they could return by another route.

"Where is your wife?" the other man asked suddenly.

This revolutionary was no fool, Red Feather realized. The man had been following the same line of thought.

"At the lodge of her father, Blue Corn," Red Feather admitted. "She visits there while we trade."

There seemed no point in lying. If he wished, this young man could quickly verify anything that Red Feather might say. He might as well speak truth.

"Good!" the young man exclaimed cheerfully. "We will wait there for you!"

Again, Red Feather burned with anger. This stranger was assuming that they would gladly turn over all they possessed to the revolutionaries. This was not the way of the People, and sooner or later, this young man would learn it. But not now. They would try to appear cooperative. There would be time to devise a plan. Start home by another way, perhaps, and then return for Moonflower. Ah, well, it would work out.

Red Feather nodded, noncommittally, and gathered his reins.

"We have far to travel," he observed. "Let us be on the trail."

The other man nodded agreement.

"We will be watching," he advised, as if to forestall any tricks.

Red Feather kneed the horse forward. An armed man stood directly in the trail, and for a moment it appeared that he would not quit his position. Then, at the last instant, the warrior seemed to glance at his leader and receive some sort of signal. Quickly, he stepped aside and the train began to file past him. Red Feather felt some sense of relief, but was tense until the last of the pack horses had passed that point. He was still angry over the presumptive arrogance of the men who had stopped them.

He looked back, and saw to his surprise that the revolutionaries had disappeared. The trail, the shady slope, the hills beyond, were again vacant of any human life.

Turkey Foot now rode forward to join him.

"What is it?" he asked seriously.

"Those are the men Blue Corn spoke of," Red Feather explained. "They hate the Spanish."

Turkey Foot nodded agreeably.

"This is understandable. What did they want with us?"

"It is very confusing, my friend. They want us to hate the Spanish, too, maybe. There is much that I do not understand."

As they rode on, Red Feather told in some detail of his conversation with Blue Corn, and of the desire of the young man to acquire the tools and weapons for which they would trade.

"No!" exclaimed the Head Splitter. "These furs belong to us. We fight, yes?"

Red Feather exhaled a deep sigh.

"It is not so simple. These are my wife's people. If we fight them, they may take vengeance on Blue Corn after we are gone."

Turkey Foot nodded again.

"Then we do not fight them. We only say, 'These things are ours.' "

"I am not sure they will understand, Turkey Foot."

"Cannot our friends, the Spanish, help? We have traded here for many seasons."

"I think not. The Spanish are hard put to defend themselves."

Turkey Foot's eyes grew round.

*"Aiee!* This is big, then!"

"Yes, it seems so."

Turkey Foot shrugged.

"Well, we will see. First, we go to Santa Fe to trade."

# About the Author
>> >> >>

**D**ON COLDSMITH was born in Iola, Kansas in 1926. He served as a World War II combat medic in the South Pacific and returned to his native state where he graduated from Baker University in 1949 and received his M.D. from the University of Kansas in 1958. He worked at several jobs before entering medical school: he was a YMCA group counselor, a gunsmith, a taxidermist, and for a short time, a Congregational preacher. In addition to his private medical practice, Dr. Coldsmith is a staff physician at Emporia State University's Health Center, teaches in the English Department, and is active as a freelance writer, lecturer, and rancher. He and his wife of 26 years, Edna, have raised five daughters.

Dr. Coldsmith produced the first ten novels in "The Spanish Bit Saga" in a five-year period; he writes and revises the stories first in his head, then in longhand. From this manuscript he reads aloud to his wife, whom he calls his "chief editor." Finally the finished version is skillfully typed by his longtime office receptionist.

Of his decision to create, or re-create, the world of the Plains Indian in the 16th and 17th centuries, the author says: "There has been very little written about this time period. I wanted also to portray these native Americans as human beings, rather than as stereotyped 'Indians.' That word does not appear anywhere in the series—for a reason. As I have researched the time and place, the indigenous cultures, it's been a truly inspiring experience for me.''

*A Proud People In a Harsh Land*

# THE SPANISH BIT SAGA

Set on the Great Plains of America in the early 16th century, Don Coldsmith's acclaimed series recreates a time, a place and a people that have been nearly lost to history. With the advent of the Spaniards, the horse culture came to the people of the Plains. Here is history in the making through the eyes of the proud Native Americans who lived it.

☐ BOOK 1: TRAIL OF THE SPANISH BIT   26397   $2.95
☐ BOOK 2: THE ELK-DOG HERITAGE   26412   $2.95
☐ BOOK 3: FOLLOW THE WIND   26806   $2.95
☐ BOOK 4: BUFFALO MEDICINE   26938   $2.95
☐ BOOK 5: MAN OF THE SHADOWS   27067   $2.95
☐ BOOK 6: DAUGHTER OF THE EAGLE   27209   $2.95
☐ BOOK 7: MOON OF THE THUNDER   27344   $2.95
☐ BOOK 8: SACRED HILLS   27460   $2.95
☐ BOOK 9: PALE STAR   27604   $2.95
☐ BOOK 10: RIVER OF SWANS   27708   $2.95
☐ BOOK 11: RETURN TO THE RIVER   28163   $2.95
☐ BOOK 12: THE MEDICINE KNIFE   28318   $2.95
☐ BOOK 13: THE FLOWER IN THE MOUNTAINS
                                                   28538   $3.50
☐ SUPER: THE CHANGING WIND   28334   $3.95

# ★ WAGONS WEST ★

This continuing, magnificent saga recounts the adventures of a brave band of settlers, all of different backgrounds, all sharing one dream—to find a new and better life.

| | | | |
|---|---|---|---|
| ☐ | 26822 | INDEPENDENCE! #1 | $4.50 |
| ☐ | 26162 | NEBRASKA! #2 | $4.50 |
| ☐ | 26242 | WYOMING! #3 | $4.50 |
| ☐ | 26072 | OREGON! #4 | $4.50 |
| ☐ | 26070 | TEXAS! #5 | $4.50 |
| ☐ | 26377 | CALIFORNIA! #6 | $4.50 |
| ☐ | 26546 | COLORADO! #7 | $4.50 |
| ☐ | 26069 | NEVADA! #8 | $4.50 |
| ☐ | 26163 | WASHINGTON! #9 | $4.50 |
| ☐ | 26073 | MONTANA! #10 | $4.50 |
| ☐ | 26184 | DAKOTA! #11 | $4.50 |
| ☐ | 26521 | UTAH! #12 | $4.50 |
| ☐ | 26071 | IDAHO! #13 | $4.50 |
| ☐ | 26367 | MISSOURI! #14 | $4.50 |
| ☐ | 27141 | MISSISSIPPI! #15 | $4.50 |
| ☐ | 25247 | LOUISIANA! #16 | $4.50 |
| ☐ | 25622 | TENNESSEE! #17 | $4.50 |
| ☐ | 26022 | ILLINOIS! #18 | $4.50 |
| ☐ | 26533 | WISCONSIN! #19 | $4.50 |
| ☐ | 26849 | KENTUCKY! #20 | $4.50 |
| ☐ | 27065 | ARIZONA! #21 | $4.50 |
| ☐ | 27458 | NEW MEXICO! #22 | $4.50 |
| ☐ | 27703 | OKLAHOMA! #23 | $4.50 |
| ☐ | 28180 | CELEBRATION! #24 | $4.50 |